JUST BECAUSE THEY CLAIM YOU, DOESN'T MAKE YOU THEIRS

USA TODAY BESTSELLING AUTHOR

REBEKAH R. GANIERE

ISBN: 978-1-63300-087-2
ISBN: 978-1-63300-091-9

All ARTWORK by VWZDesigns.com

DEDICATION

To those who Read, and to those who Love, and those who love to do both.

CHAPTER ONE

RIVER

"Did you take your medicine?"

River rolled her eyes. Every month, Cherry asked the same question, and every month since she'd been twelve, the answer had been the same.

"River?" Cherry wouldn't be ignored.

River looked up from her bowl of cereal and stared at her mom. "You know, I'm twenty-one now. Do you need to keep making me feel like I'm five?"

Cherry set down her cup of coffee and leveled her gaze on River.

That gaze had stopped working on River long ago, but with everything they had going on, River didn't want to give her mom any more reason to freak out.

"Yes, Mom, I took it. You know I took it. I saw you go through my trash, looking for the empty bottle. So you know I took one every day this month."

Like clockwork, Cherry emptied River's trash at the end of the first day of the month. And Cherry didn't take the bag to the pack burn pile. Cherry put that trash with the glass bottle in the back of the old Corolla and drove it into town to dispose of, away from the pack.

River wondered for the millionth time why the hell her medicine made Cherry such a freak. But ever since the first time at age twelve when River had thought she would die, River never again refused to take the medicine. She figured Cherry didn't want anyone to know about it because something was wrong with River. River didn't know what, but it made Cherry both fearful and ashamed.

Cherry had never once let River run with the pack at the full moon. She'd never even let River shift in front of anyone except for her and Bianca and Strider on a few occasions. Those times had been on Bianca's first few shifts. Cherry and Strider had packed the girls into the Corolla and driven them back to where Cherry and River had lived with River's dad before he'd died. The four ran together in the abandoned pack grounds, teaching River and Bianca everything they needed to know to survive as wolves.

River always knew something was different about her and her wolf. Pack members talk about their bonds with their wolves. They made them seem like an extension of themselves, whereas River only ever connected with her wolf when she'd run with Cherry and Strider. There'd never been fights for control. No wolf emerging at the height of strong emotions. No cravings. No needing. And most of all, no heats. As far as River could tell, she was damaged, and everyone knew it. It was the only explanation for why her mom never let her shift or run with anyone outside her family.

"Have you showered?" Cherry asked.

River shook her head.

"Do it. This is the annual meeting. Not only our pack will be there-"

"All the packs across the state will be there. Yes, Mom. I am aware. Bianca won't stop talking about it."

Mating runs happened every full moon. But once a year, all the packs in the state got together for a run. Hundreds of unmated shifters showed up. To River, it was the most depressing of all runs. Seeing so many shifters with looks ranging from hope to complete desperation put River on edge.

At age twenty-five, if a shifter hadn't found their mate, they were ejected from their packs to find their mate elsewhere. They were only allowed to return if they found a mate. Most never returned, however. Seriously, who would want to go back to live with people who had tossed you out in your most significant time of need? Packs were more than neighbors; they were supposed to be family. Losing the connection with their packs sent most unmated shifters into a complete tailspin. The loss of family, connection, support, and, most of all, comfort. She'd heard of more than one shifter taking their own life to end the pain. Worse yet were the ones who fell into drugs to dull the pain. Would that be her fate?

"We need to be at the mating run in two hours. Hurry and shower and change into something nice."

Nice. Not comfortable. Not easy to shift in. Nice. For five years, River had gone to the mating runs wearing something nice. Other females wore soft, easy-to-remove clothes meant for shifting out of. But not River. Never River. Why? Because River never found a mate. Hell, the males barely noticed her, not that she cared. There wasn't one of them who had ever caught her eye. Even the Alpha's son Zade. Every other female in the pack had vied for his attention, primping and preening whenever he came within eyesight, but not River. River couldn't care less about the cocky jock.

In high school, he'd been the all-American favorite. But to River, he'd been like everyone else. Sometimes, River pondered if she was asexual. But in the end, she didn't care. All she wanted was to work on her art and keep to herself.

"River, did you hear me?"

River slammed her spoon into her bowl. "Yes, Cherry. I heard you."

Cherry growled. She opened her mouth, closed it again, and slammed her coffee mug into the sink.

Maybe River cared more about finding a mate than she realized.

"Problem?" Strider entered the kitchen, his eyes darting between them.

Cherry snatched her leather coat and slung it over her shoulders. Strider kissed her head, but Cherry's gaze remained locked on River.

"Spray yourself before you come," she said. "Extra spray since there are other packs."

River fought the urge to roll her eyes and simply nodded.

Cherry kissed Strider and walked toward the door. "I gotta meet with the Alpha."

Strider nodded. "We'll see you there."

Cherry exited the house without another word, and Strider looked at River.

"She doesn't mean to be like that. You know how she gets at the mating runs. She has a lot of responsibility."

River poked her bowl of mushy cereal. "Why do I have to go?

It's not like anyone is going to want me. No one new has moved into the pack since us. And I am sure there won't be anyone new, either. And if there are, they will either be way younger than me or a rogue."

Strider walked to her and hugged her shoulder. "It's tradition, sweetheart. As long as you are in the pack, it's required."

"Yeah, well, maybe I should move away."

Strider stiffened. "Don't say that."

River shrugged. "I found a school in New York City. An art school. They have an amazing program."

Strider stared at her for a long moment. "You've already made up your mind, haven't you?"

River looked into her stepfather's soft brown eyes and nodded. He was so like her father, but not at the same time. They were both kind and diplomatic, but where her dad had been loud and fun, Strider was quiet and content to let her mom lead in every way.

Strider blew out a breath. "Does your mother know?"

River snorted.

He touched her shoulder. "Let's talk about it tomorrow. For today, let's get through this."

"Okay."

A squeal sounded behind her, and River's younger stepsister, Bianca, jogged into the room.

"What do you think?" she asked River, twisting from side to side and showing off her new jogging suit. "Dad got it for me. Cute, right?"

Strider smiled affectionately, making her heart squeeze. Her dad used to look at her like that.

"Super cute." River hopped off her barstool, dumped out her cereal, and put the bowl in the dishwasher.

"Are you gonna get ready?" Bianca bounced with energy.

"Yup. Doing it now."

Bianca bounced from foot to foot. "Well, hurry up. I want to be early and check out the males."

River couldn't help but smile. "It's the same guys we've seen for the last million years."

Bianca gripped River's hands. "Maybe this will be my year. I'll see one of them, and it will be like seeing them for the first time, and our wolves will connect."

River hoped it happened for Bianca. The girl had been dreaming about her mate for as long as she could talk.

River put on a smile. "I hope this is your year, sis."

Bianca hugged River. "I'll wait for you."

River walked through the narrow hall to her room and opened the door. She scanned the room with walls plastered in various art pieces she'd cut from magazines, printed from the internet, and taken photos of on trips into New York City with her mom.

She would miss her little room when she moved away for school, but she couldn't hang around the pack and continue to let Strider and Cherry pay her way for the rest of their lives. Her dad may have been an Alpha, but that legacy and respect only went so far for a female wolf with no mate or purpose in the pack.

She stripped off her pajamas and tossed them to the floor before wrapping in a towel and heading for the shower. She wanted to get the day over with and tell her mom she was leaving to focus on her future.

RIVER WALKED TO THE CAMP CENTER WITH STRIDER AND BIANCA. Bianca chattered and bounced around more than usual with frenzied excitement. River bore it patiently, smiling and nodding but not listening. Nervousness about talking to her mom about art school tied her in knots.

All around, scents of all the newcomers permeated the air. Unmated males and females of age milled about, chatting and laughing nervously. Their pack wasn't the biggest in the northeast, not by a long shot, but there were still close to fifty pack members, and with all the others who had shown up, there had to be two hundred unmated shifters out there.

A handful of males and females prowled the edges of the meeting spot with wild eyes. The sight made River's heart squeeze. The rogues. Some looked desperate, while others appeared like they might snap and claim anyone without permission. Those were the ones River worried about most. Not for herself; she was her mother's daughter and handled herself with no problem. But for Bianca. As much as River loved her, Bianca could be an airhead, and if one of those rogues cornered her, there was no telling what would happen. Of course, one of those rogues would have to be insane to try and do something to Cherry's stepdaughter. Her mom would rip out their heart with her bare hands and eat it while it still beat.

A bark resounded through the air, and the group quieted. Bianca kissed Strider and ran over to join the group of unmated.

Their Alpha jumped on one of the picnic benches, and everyone in attendance bowed. He reached down, took his mate's hand, and gently pulled her beside him. Their pack Luna, Kawli, was one of the gentlest women River had met. Never once had River seen her angry or raise her voice. She was the calm to their Alpha's storm.

"Welcome," he said. "Tonight is our annual mating gathering, and I welcome everyone who has traveled to be here. We will begin with the run, followed by a meal, and finally, the sealing of all new matings."

The shifters howled, and the air electrified it with anticipation. She knew from experience the scents of every unmated shifter would rise with each minute. Her mother and Strider had taught her and Bianca how to control their senses so as not to become overwhelmed by them. Their sense of smell, hearing, sight, and more. River knew when to block them out and when to use them. River perked up her hearing and eyesight but clamped down her sense of smell to keep her brain from fogging over with all the pheromones flying around.

River gazed into the sky. The sun would set in the next hour, and the matings would begin as soon as it did. No one knew precisely why the moon held so much sway over their wolves, but the lunar cycles had been tied to shifters for as long as there had been shifters. They purposely picked a non-full moon night to hold runs for that reason. Currently, the moon was in its waning gibbous phase. The full moon had passed a week ago, and while in the waning gibbous phase, shifters were as docile and reasonable as they would ever be.

"It's starting," Strider whispered.

River tore her eyes back to the group as they began shifting, and part of her hoped something would happen with her wolf. As much as she hated that part of herself, she couldn't help it. Every time, the same thing happened. She wished and hoped for something to happen with her wolf. For her to wake up. Howl. Demand to be let free. Something, anything. But nothing ever happened. Nothing. Not a shot. Not a tingle. Not a twinge. She peered at the moon again. Was she even an actual shifter? She would seriously question her biology if she didn't have her enhanced senses and hadn't run with her mom and Strider before.

"I'm gonna go help prep the food."

Strider caught her hand.

She stopped, knowing what would come next. It had been like this every time. The sadness in his eyes at the fact that she hadn't found a mate. That she hadn't felt a twitch or twinge of desire for anyone. Ever. That she would remain alone until the pack kicked her out.

"I'll pay for art school," Strider blurted.

River stared at him. Had she heard him right? "What?"

"I'll pay for it. Whatever it costs. You figure out a plan and give it to me, and I'll talk to your mom."

River's mouth fell open. She liked Strider, even loved him, but she'd always kept him at arm's length because letting him in would somehow be disloyal to her father. Though for the last decade, Strider had been there for every moment of her life.

"I… Strider-"

He pulled her in and hugged her. "There's more to life than a fated mate, River. And I want you to find what you want for yourself."

She didn't know what to say.

An Alpha howl shook the trees, and Strider let go of her. "I have to chaperone."

River nodded, unable to form words. As Strider shifted and jogged down to the group, River smiled and turned toward the food kitchen.

It was going to happen. She would go to art school. A warmth of joy spread through her body, and as much as she didn't want to get excited, she couldn't help the skip that made its way into her step as she went off to peel potatoes. And Strider was right. There was more to life than a fated mate. Her mom and dad had been fated mates, and it hadn't gone well.

River peeled fifty pounds of potatoes with an ancient metal peeler that made her grip ache. Mates of other pack members helped prep food for when everyone returned. They would stroll back, starving, sweating, and stinking of sex. And it would be her cue to duck out and head back to her house. She breathed the fresh air, knowing it would be one of the last she would get for days. The afterscents of mating runs clung to every leaf in the woods.

She briefly shut her eyes and envisioned herself running with the pack like a wolf. Her eyes locking with some handsome timber wolf and then the heart-bursting unity which came from finding her mate. They would move toward each other, unable to resist the pull. Their wolves would demand to be unleashed together before the unbridled sex started. What would that be like?

She opened her eyes and peered into the darkness beyond. A light breeze blew in through the window, and a fragrance slammed into her. River stopped peeling and stiffened. The scent of honey and amber surrounded her, and for the first time, her wolf lifted her head and whined.

River's potato plopped into the sink, and she backed away so quick she slipped and landed on the floor with a thud.

"River, are you okay?" asked her Luna.

"What is it?" asked another mate she didn't recognize.

The women stopped talking, and one of them shut off the radio, making the kitchen eerily quiet except for the sounds of food cooking.

"Do you smell it?" one of the women asked.

"What are they doing here?" said another mate shakily.

"They weren't invited," another whispered.

"Screw invited," said a fourth woman. "They make the rules. They can go where they want."

"We need to get the Alpha," said the first.

River's heart beat louder, and her wolf stood. What the hell? The scent grew more potent, and one of the women yanked River away from the back door.

When had she walked to the back door?

River's wolf lurched forward, and River doubled over, pain ripping through her. She screamed and gripped the potato peeler so hard she thought it might jam through her hand.

"River? River, what's wrong?" asked someone in a faraway voice.

River panted, and pain ripped through her again.

"I... I think River is shifting," someone called.

A woman knelt next to River, and through bleary eyes, River barely made out her Luna, Kawli.

No. No. No. Her mom would kill her. She needed to get out of there. Needed to get away. They couldn't see her. Cherry would kill her if they saw her shift.

"Everyone in the pantry," Kawli yelled.

"River, come on." Kawli dragged her backward.

The ripple stopped, and River took a breath. "I need to go home."

"No time," said Kawli. "They are coming. You need to hide. You are unmated, River."

Who? Who's coming?

The fragrance grew more potent, and River's wolf shook her

head. River experienced her wolf's confusion. A mix of recognition swirled with fear.

Fear? Great. Her wolf decided to wake up just to be afraid. *Lovely.*

The women hurried into the pantry, dragging River with them. As they began closing the door, the back door's handle turned, and the wood swung inward.

The women huddled in the corner behind heavy metal shelves, but River couldn't bring herself to. She looked from them to the door and back again. Why were they so scared? She practically saw their heads hung and tails secured between their legs. Even Kawli moved to join the other women.

Her gaze swung back to the door, and her wolf growled. A ripple tugged at her gut again, but River quashed it. There was something else, though… something her wolf couldn't quite place. That scent… honey and amber… so invading, so masculine, so…

Heavy footsteps prowled to the pantry door.

"Ron," one of the women whispered into her phone. The woman whined. "Ronny."

A growl sounded through the phone, followed by yelling from the other end. Ron, one of the pack's Betas, let out an emergency danger howl that cut through the night outside.

What the hell was going on?

River's wolf scratched to be loose, but River refused to let the bitch take over. No way her wolf was emerging because of some male.

Something sharp dragged across the pantry door, and the handle turned. The door creaked open.

River's wolf paced back and forth, becoming more and more agitated. A second later, the door opened fully, flooding the dark room with light and silhouetting the largest male River had seen. In wolf form, he stood almost five feet tall. His dark fur held patches of red, and his yellow eyes remained alert and terrifying.

A rogue. It had to be a rogue. But she'd never seen one so enormous before. He sniffed before growling.

River's wolf snarled and paced.

Something wasn't right with him. He seemed… feral.

The wolf stepped forward, and River brandished the potato peeler she still gripped.

Awesome, what was she going to do? Peel him to death?

Haha. Maybe it'll make him more appealing. She fought a snicker. Why did she always laugh at the worst times?

She should have been scared of the newcomer but remained eerily calm for some reason. Her wolf, however, started going haywire, and for the first time, River needed to protect not only herself but also her wolf.

"Stay back," River ordered. "There are no unmated females in here." It was a lie, but hell, it was worth a try.

The wolf sniffed again and took a step forward. River slashed at him with the peeler.

"I said, stay away. Trust me, dude; you don't want to mess with any of us. My mom is the pack enforcer, and these women are all mates of the Alpha and Betas."

The air shimmered, and the man shifted to human form. He remained crouched on the floor for a moment and then lifted his head.

He was handsome. Damn handsome. Blond hair with dark eyes. Tanned skin from being outside. Heavy chiseled jaw and cheekbones. Dirt smeared his naked body. Even so, she made out clearly ripped muscles and a dozen or so scars.

"You aren't mated." He stepped forward and sniffed again.

"Doesn't mean I want you."

His odor surrounded her, mixing her wolf up even more.

The man smiled, revealing bright white teeth. "Doesn't matter. I want you, and you cannot refuse me."

Of course, she could refuse him. It was the law. He may be the best-looking guy she'd seen since the Australian Firefighters calendar on her bedroom wall, but that did not mean she would fall at his feet.

"An escape mental patient? I mean, only an insane man would say I can't refuse you. I can refuse anyone the hell I want," she answered. "Also, you'd have to be insane to come here and corner a group of mated females. If you leave now, you'll make it to the borders of our lands before the rest of our pack chases you down."

He took another step forward. "I smell you, wolf. You can hide all you want behind desensitizers with shifters, but not with me. I'm Lycan and an Alpha's son. Lycans take what they want. And I want you."

The man covered the distance between them in one long stride.

She backed up as he pounced and wrapped his arms around her. The women behind her screamed as River fell to the floor, the man crouched over her. He pinned her to the ground with his tremendous weight.

His eyes flashed blue, then yellow, and finally black. "Mine. Omega."

For a split second, everything slowed as he took her in. Her wolf quieted, and they both watched emotions play all over his face. His eyes morphed back and forth between colors as if he couldn't decide what he wanted to be.

Omega? What did he mean Omega? She wasn't an Omega. She wasn't anything.

River opened her mouth to say something, but a sharp pain pierced her throat.

River blinked, frozen in place as her wolf roared to life.

Bitten. He'd bitten her. He'd marked her. The icy chill of violation rained down on her.

No. No. No. Her wolf howled and snarled and fought against the restraint that appeared like a long red rope and snagged one of her legs.

Bonding. He was trying to bond with her.

A commotion sounded behind them, and Cherry roared. River's wolf whimpered as the red rope snaked up her leg.

River. Help.

The sound of her wolf's voice made River jerk to life. Rage burst through River like an explosion, and she roared and unpinned her right hand. She jammed the peeler downward into the male's back. His teeth disengaged from her throat, and he howled in pain. Again, River stabbed him. And a third time, reaching for his neck. Blood spurted from the wounds and splashed her face and arms.

Angry hands yanked the male off her.

"You son of a bitch! I'm going to rip your teeth out!" Cherry screamed.

River lay dazed for a minute before Strider rushed in. "River. Sweetheart. Are you okay?"

She fought to speak as her wolf squirmed in the red rope, howling and crying.

Strider inspected her. "Are you hurt? Is the blood his or yours?"

She fought to make coherent sentences, unable to process as the screams of her wolf echoed in her head.

Strider shook her gently. "River! Did he bite you?"

His voice pierced her brain fog, and she lifted her hand to her throat. A gash tore through her throat, spurting blood as skin dangled to the side.

"Shit." He picked her up and carried her out of the pantry, laying her on the counter. The other pack leaders rushed in and yelled for their mates. The noise and commotion overwhelmed her as dozens of people entered the kitchen.

Cherry appeared at her side. "What happened?"

River tried to use the edge of her sundress to staunch the bleeding in her neck. She healed as quickly as the next wolf, but she'd need stitches anyway.

Strider looked at Cherry and then River. "He bit her."

Terror flashed across Cherry's face, and she focused on River. "Do you see her?" she demanded. "Your wolf. Do you see her?"

River couldn't do more than nod.

"Is there a rope? Is she tethered to a rope?"

River nodded again. "It's red," she managed.

Cherry roared and pulled a gun from her back pocket. "He bit her! He bit her against her will!" She ran to where no less than a dozen pack members restrained the now bleeding and feral-looking male. "I'm gonna blow your f-ing head off, you son of a bitch." Cherry cocked the hammer of her gun, but as it went off, their Alpha pushed the gun out of the way. The bullet missed the male by less than an inch.

Cherry whirled on the Alpha and pointed the gun straight in his face. The Alpha told Cherry to drop the weapon.

"He bit my daughter. He tried to claim her without consent. He deserves death."

The Alpha remained calm. "Yes. But that's not our place to decide."

Cherry glared at the male and back at their Alpha. "He's a

rogue. No one will miss him. He dies for the violation of my daughter." Cherry raised the gun and pulled the trigger a second time, but this time, their Alpha moved so fast River barely saw the blur. The bullet struck the male in the shoulder, but Cherry flew across the kitchen and smacked the wall with a crack. Strider growled and rushed to her.

"Enough," the Alpha roared. A wave of Alpha aura shot through the room, making everyone drop to one knee. Everyone except for River and her mother. Not that River could have gotten to her knees unless she fell off the counter.

The Alpha stared hard at Cherry, and Cherry knelt next to Strider.

The Alpha turned his attention to River and sniffed the air. His eyes narrowed, and he called to her. "River, come here."

She sat up shakily but didn't experience the pull to obey everyone else did. Expressions of confusion surrounded her, and a murmur and several small gasps sounded around her.

"River," the Alpha commanded.

She'd never felt the compulsion everyone else did. Her mom had always told her to pretend, but in light of what had happened and that their Alpha wasn't willing to kill the Lycan who had bitten her, she decided not to pretend any longer. Her wolf snarled and fought the red rope. She didn't like the Lycan being allowed to live any more than River or Cherry did.

River walked to the Alpha, and he peered into her eyes for the first time in her life.

River never knew why her mom had told her to stay away from the pack Alpha and his Betas, but she hadn't argued. She'd always figured it had to do with being unable to compel River with their commands, but now, looking into his eyes, there was more to it.

The Alpha inspected her and sniffed again. His eyes narrowed and went Alpha golden. What was he looking at?

She moved her shredded sundress to the side, exposing the bite, which had already stopped bleeding but remained open and raw.

"You have two choices," he said. "You can allow his marking to stand and go with him or reject him."

Cherry stood, but Strider pulled her back down and whispered to her.

River's wolf strained against the rope.

Not. Him. Hurt. Forced. Not. Him.

River fixed her eyes on the still handsome but bloodied male and then at her Alpha. "Not him," she repeated.

The Alpha nodded and ushered River forward until her knees connected with the male's.

"Tell him," said the Alpha. "Reject him. It's the only way to break the bond and free your wolf."

River's mouth dried as the crazed look faded from the male's face, and instead, fear replaced it as he blinked at her. His eyes went from black to a beautiful blue. Gone was the beast who had come into the pantry. Gone was the man who had bitten her. Replaced by the face of a terrified, desperate man.

No! He'd bitten her. He'd taken from her one of the only things wolves never took. *Agency.*

She swallowed hard, but her throat stuck together like she'd drunk super glue.

A Lycan Alpha had tried to mate her. He'd called her his. His Omega.

Terror flooded River, and her body shook. Everyone knew about the Lycans. The elder purebloods of her race. The original werewolves. Bigger. Faster. Filthy rich and utter killing machines. But Lycans didn't live in the States; they lived in Canada and Europe. So, what was a Lycan doing there? And why was an Alpha Lycan a rogue?

"Tell him," her mom commanded. "Tell him you reject him, River."

River regarded her mom and then the male. His scent invaded her again- sweet and musky.

"I..." Why did an Alpha Lycan want her?

He roared and pulled against the men holding him, and his gaze connected with hers again, but this time, there wasn't anger, only pain.

"Don't," he pleaded. "Please."

Those two words crashed down around her like the emotion in his eyes, and she paused.

Her wolf howled. *Not. This. One.*

The pain and pleading in her wolf's voice spurred River into action.

She let her grip on her wolf slip, and her claws extended and swiped straight across his handsome face, slicing it open from ear to cheekbone. "Not. You."

Anger seared in her bright as the red rope tethering her wolf. The bite in her neck burned like ice.

"I reject you," she whispered.

His eyes went wide, and they both stopped breathing as the rope unwound from her wolf, leaving behind a patch of missing fur where it had first snaked around her leg.

He sucked in a breath before roaring and breaking free from the men. He lunged at River, but she held out the peeler again.

"I said, I reject you!"

She had no idea where the strength had come from, nor the command in her voice, but somehow it made the male stop.

His eyes flashed, and emotions played all over his face for a moment. He reached for her but stopped. His expression changed to one of pain and utter loneliness.

"I'm sorry, Omega. I'm so sorry," he whispered before fleeing out the door.

River shook from adrenaline, and everything stood still before she fell to the floor. Her mother rushed to her and grabbed onto River. Strider followed suit, and the whole room of shifters stared at them.

Cherry released her. "Are you okay? Is your wolf okay?"

River nodded. "Mom? Why did he call me Omega?"

"Yes, Cherry," said the Alpha. "I think you better tell all of us."

CHAPTER TWO

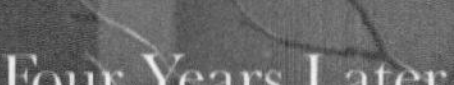

Four Years Later

RIVER

River turned off her torch and inspected her sculpture. The wolf's head was complete. She'd spent days trying to bend his spine right and make him as realistic as possible while he leapt off the rock. And now, with the head finished... she smiled. It was how she imagined her father's wolf.

River's phone rang, and she glanced at it.

Bianca.

She'd not seen her little sister in three months, which was about as long as she'd spent tied to her workshop sculpting.

"Hey, Sis."

Bianca squealed in delight, and River held the phone away from her ear. She spoke so fast that River fought to keep up. The only words River caught for sure were mating run, fated mate, ultra-sexy, and super-rich. The rest, River guessed.

It had been four years since the night when she'd been attacked and found out the truth. She'd heard about Omegas before. How special and unique they were, and how they were the only true mates of Lycan Alphas. And more than that, only a handful had been born in the last hundred years. Unfortunately, since Omegas were so rare and securely guarded by the Alphas who wanted them, little was known to shifters about them.

The night of the last mating run River had attended, the Alpha himself had taken River and put her in an apartment safehouse the pack owned in the nearest city. River hadn't known about the safe house until that night.

In fear the Lycan and the others he had brought would come back for her, every wolf at the mating run was ordered to scour the acreage between the pack village and the major surrounding cities, though they weren't told why. They marked every yard with their scents to try and mask River's. Strider had gotten her an apartment and signed her up for art school within a week. Then, he and Cherry had taken River to New York to start school the following month.

Her mom had burned all of River's belongings. And in the end, their house out of paranoia. She, Strider, and Bianca had moved into a new house several miles from the old one. Though River hadn't been there, she'd seen photos. It hadn't been as spacious as their home together, but Cherry and Strider had never been ones to prize material things- even though Strider had inherited money years earlier.

Bianca's rambling pulled River back to the present. She rubbed her forehead and switched her phone to the other hand.

"Bianca… Bianca… Bianca!"

Her sister stopped talking. "What?"

"I'm happy for you, sis. I am. Have Cherry and Strider met him yet?"

"No. I want you to meet him first."

A small surge of panic lit inside River. "But weren't they at the mating run?"

"Uh…" Bianca hesitated.

River scrunched up her face. "What did you do?"

"Nothing bad," she said. "A couple of the other unmated girls and I heard about a gathering up north, and we decided to check it out."

"Bianca!" River's heart raced.

Her wolf woke up and whined.

It's all right, girl. She's fine. We're fine.

"It's perfectly safe," said Bianca. "A dozen Alphas were there, and everything went perfectly."

River rubbed her head.

"So, will you?"

"Will I what?"

"Meet him. I need you on my side before I tell Mom and Dad. They won't be happy I went; you know how Cherry is. She's likely to rip Zeke a new one before she gets to know him."

"Zeke?"

"Yeah, that's his name. Please?" Bianca drew out the word like a pouting high schooler.

"B, I'm super busy. I have my show this weekend and-"

"I haven't seen you in months. Ever since you left… I… I need you. Please?" Bianca's voice cracked.

She'd seen little of her family since the move to the city. Cherry was always on alert for the possibility of Lycans finding River. So, she hadn't allowed River to visit home in four years. They'd come to the city every six months since she'd moved and for her graduation from art school. Other than that, she'd been alone in the city.

A war had started amongst the Lycans in the last years since she'd been bitten. They'd divided for the first time in hundreds of years. Lycans had recruited the strongest werewolves from the States to join their ranks, turning them into Lycan hybrids. They weren't true Lycans, but they inherited the Lycan strength, speed, and agility. There was a lot they still didn't know about the new Lycan hybrids. One thing had been for certain, though: hybrids were not attracted to Omegas the way Alphas and Lycans were, which was why, after recruiting the new hybrids, the first thing they'd been sent to do was search for Omegas- causing Cherry to double her efforts to keep River's identity secret.

Word had gotten out about River somehow, and the search had begun. Which was the only reason she'd continued to take the suppression pills and desensitizing spray her mom had forced her to take since turning twelve.

"River, you aren't listening, are you?"

River sucked in a breath.

"We won't come to you. We can meet somewhere you choose. Somewhere safe. And I'll make sure to do all the protocols afterward. I'll take everything off when I'm back at my hotel. I'll wash it all in the special soap. I'll take a shower and everything. And since I'm staying in a hotel, they'll bleach the hell out of all my sheets, towels, and everything. If I have to, I'll spray myself with the scent-neutralizer stuff."

"And what about your new mate? What are you going to tell him about all your weird protocols?"

"Nothing. We aren't fully bonded yet, and until we are, I won't tell him anything about you."

Bianca didn't know the full extent of River's status. She knew River had been attacked and marked by a rogue without consent and that she'd left for her safety. The only people who knew her identity as an Omega were Cherry, Strider, her pack leaders, and their mates who had witnessed the attack. And, of course, the asshole who had bitten her. His penetrating eyes invaded her mind.

"Don't. Please." His voice echoed in her head.

River had never once regretted rejecting him. But ever since he'd woken up her wolf, her wolf had become increasingly agitated with River's lack of desire to find an Alpha to mate.

Damn. River could use a break, and she did miss Bianca. Going to school and getting a job at a prestigious art gallery had been a dream for River, but she'd never felt so utterly alone before. Even the occasional comfort of her wolf hadn't been enough to replace her pack.

"When are you going to try to move forward?" Bianca asked in a small voice. "It's been four years."

River never talked to Bianca about what had happened. Hell, she'd never spoken to anyone about it except Cherry and Strider. But that had only been because they needed to tell her the truth.

"Hello? River, I'm sorry. I shouldn't have said that."

"Yeah." She shook her head to clear her thoughts. "B, it would take me forever to get ready. By the time I finished and got to dinner, it would be so late-"

"I don't care. Zeke won't either. I just want you to meet him. We'll take you somewhere nice. Super nice. Quadruple nice. Thousand-dollar bottle of champagne nice. And we'll pay for everything, and it'll be-"

"Nice?" River blurted. "Okay. Okay. I'll go."

"Wahoo! You go take a shower, and I'll set up everything."

"Setup?" River's stomach plummeted to her toes.

"Yeah. I'll be there in twenty minutes. I'm a few miles away. Love ya, Sis."

Before River replied, Bianca hung up.

"Shit." Not good.

River groaned and hung up. She ran her hand over the smooth metal and smiled. Hell knew she needed a good… time. She'd never been the one-night stand type, but even her favorite personal toy in her nightstand had burned out from overuse. She took the wolfsbane extract to keep her heats at bay like Cherry had taught her, but they'd never again gone away completely since being bitten by the rogue.

She'd done a ton of research in the last four years. The best advice she'd found was that when her heat cycle hit, she should take cool baths, use ice packs, and see how fast she could wear out the batteries in her little gang of vibrators. Her previous heat cycle had lasted five days, and she'd gone through a hundred dollars' worth of toys and three hundred dollars' worth of batteries. She couldn't imagine what a real heat cycle would be like. Oh, wait, yes, she could; the memory of her first cycle burned into her skull and was one of the things that kept her remembering to take her suppressors and scent-blocking spray.

River peeled off her gloves and apron and trudged to the spray nozzle hanging in the corner. Bianca was right. She deserved a night off. She'd been working so much she'd barely had time to sleep over the past month.

She removed her overalls and stepped under the chilly spray. It pelted her skin like tiny missiles and made her nipples pucker. The urge to go up to her loft and take a proper shower trickled over her, but as the water went from warm to hot, the idea of running across her workshop naked and freezing was not half as appealing.

River leaned against the cement wall, letting her head fall beneath the spray. Damn, that felt amazing. She hadn't realized how tense her muscles had gotten until they started relaxing. How many hours had she been in the shop? Eight? Ten? Nope. Fourteen. She'd been working for fourteen hours. No wonder she ached all over.

Her mind wandered to places she didn't want it to go, but as she fought against the lull of sleep, she couldn't stop the memories from flooding back.

"Mom, it hurts so bad." River quaked in her bed as Cherry paced back and forth.

"Shit. Shit. Shit. Shit. Shit."

River's body trembled as another cramp ripped through her and shot straight to her core. She was dying. Why wasn't her mom doing anything? Did she want her to die?

River whimpered.

Cherry sprayed another round of air freshener and checked to ensure the window remained shut and locked and that the towels she'd shoved into the cracks hadn't moved.

River cried out as another wave of sharp pains shot through her.

Cherry sat on the side of River's bed and patted her leg. "It's gonna be okay, River. I'm gonna take care of everything."

The hell she was. So far, her mom had stunk up the room like flowers and made sure no one else knew she was dying.

"Do you hate me this much?" River barely got the words out without vomiting due to the overwhelming sweet floral scent.

Cherry didn't answer right away. "I... I don't hate you, River. I'm trying to help you, I promise. You don't understand right now-"

"If you wanted to help me, you'd take me to the pack doctor. Dad would do it. Dad would take me." River said accusingly.

Cherry opened and closed her mouth several times and turned away.

River stared at her mom through burning eyes so dry she feared they'd crack.

Cherry brushed her hand across her face and stood again. A soft knock on the door pulled Cherry's attention, and she ran to it.

"Yeah?"

"It's me," came a muffled voice from the other side.

"Did you find it?" The frenzy in her mother's voice was something River hadn't heard before. Her mom was the cool one. The strong one. The non-emotional one. Cherry was your girl if you needed something done or someone smacked into line.

"Yes," came the reply.

Cherry moved the towel out from under the door and kicked aside the blanket she'd stapled around River's door before unlocking and opening it no more than a crack.

An arm shot through the door holding several items River couldn't make out, and then the door shut.

"River?" came the small, scared voice of her little sister Bianca through the door. "I want River."

Her stepfather Strider must have said something to Bianca because she began to cry and bang on the door.

"Something's wrong with her. I can smell it. Mama Cherry let me in," Bianca cried.

Strider said something else in a low voice, and Bianca's small hand stopped banging on the door. Her sobbing lessened as Strider moved her away from the room.

River willed Bianca to run. To go to their Alpha or a Beta or anyone to get her help, but it wouldn't happen. Bianca would never go against what her father said. As much as her little sister loved her, she loved her dad more.

Cherry approached the bed as another round of cramps ripped through River. Cherry brought over the dark amber bottle Strider had given her and opened it.

"You need to drink this."

Die. She wanted to die. River groaned as Cherry pressed the bottle toward her lips.

River twisted away as her stomach roiled.

"Stop. You need to drink this, River. You have to. Please."

River peered at her mom through bleary eyes. She'd never once heard her mom say please for anything.

"I promise I'm trying to help." Cherry's voice shook.

River sat against her pillow, her body slick with sweat and her sheets so soaked that she feared she might slide right off the bed.

She'd never been sick a day in her life; shifters rarely if ever, got sick. But this…

River opened her mouth, and Cherry poured the liquid into it. River gagged at the bitter taste and almost spit it out, but Cherry shut her lips. The liquid burned, and River shook her head.

"Swallow it, River," her mom commanded.

Poison. Cherry was trying to poison her.

River fought against her mom, but Cherry was strong- the strongest female River had ever known. Even so, Cherry seemed to have trouble keeping River from overpowering her.

"Dammit, River, I'm trying to help you. Swallow the fucking liquid."

River didn't stop fighting, so Cherry jumped on her, pinned her down with her legs, and held River's nose.

Dead. Cherry wanted her dead.

Another wave of sharp pains shot through River's core, and she swallowed the liquid as the lack of oxygen made her head fuzz over.

River waited for the searing pain to shoot through her again, but like a wave crashing on the rocks, the pain dissipated, and the sharpness lost its edge. Within a minute, the burning in her mouth subsided, and her throat numbed.

Cherry released her, and River gulped in the air. Cherry watched her for several seconds, breathing heavily.

"I told you I wasn't trying to hurt you."

River touched the inside of her mouth with her tongue. It felt coated and strange.

"You need to take the rest." Cherry shoved the bottle at River.

River lifted a shaky hand, and another wave of pain built in her core, but not as intense as previously.

River closed her eyes and chugged the rest of the bottle, forcing herself to swallow it.

Again, the pain crested and dissipated, but nowhere near as painful as it had been.

Cherry kept her eyes on River. River sucked in several breaths and fell against her pillow.

Her body felt like she'd sprinted the whole pack woods for hours without stopping.

She handed the empty bottle back to Cherry, and her body went limp. Sleep. She needed sleep.

Cherry touched River's forehead and then stood. She walked to River's dresser and picked up a set of sheets and several blankets. She brought them back and sat them on the floor before pulling out a bottle and syringe.

The clear liquid filled the syringe, and Cherry approached her and rolled River's soaked T-shirt sleeve up.

She plunged the needle into River's arm, but compared to what River had been through, it felt like no more than a bee sting.

River's eyelids grew heavy as her body relaxed further.

Cherry brushed her lips across River's hair as sleep pulled River further into unconsciousness.

"Sleep now, River. Mommy is going to take care of everything. I promise."

"RIVER? RIVER!"

River opened her eyes with a start. Cool water pelted her skin. Crap, how long had she been under the spray?

"River?"

She turned to find Bianca standing in her workshop, holding a black bag.

"Are you okay?"

River nodded and turned off the water.

"Sorry," said River. "I didn't hear you come in."

Bianca tossed her towel at her. "We have reservations in thirty minutes. We need to hurry."

River nodded and toweled off. Her stomach grumbled.

"Oh, girl, you are all skin and bones. Have you eaten this month?" Bianca asked behind her.

River located underwear and pulled them on before turning toward her sister. "Is that supposed to make me feel better or make you feel better about yourself?"

Bianca laughed and shrugged. "Both."

Bianca had always had a sexy hourglass figure. Like she'd lived in a waist cincher for years. But nope. Those were Bianca's natural assets. River, on the other hand, was petite and slender like her mom. But that didn't mean a damn thing she'd learned early on. She may be little and thin, but she sure packed a punch. Or a kick. And with knives, she was deadly.

Bianca tossed River a bra and marched up to River's loft. "Come on. We don't have much time, and I have a lot to accomplish."

River groaned and shook her head. Maybe she shouldn't have said yes to Bianca.

Bianca held up the huge cup she'd been hiding behind her back. "Come on, Miss Grumpy. I brought your favorite."

River couldn't help but smile.

Bianca shook the cup. "I'll let you have it like a good girl if you let me do your hair."

River shook her head and followed her sister. She had to fix her addiction to caffeine and sugar. It was sad that with a massive cola, she could be talked into doing about anything.

AFTER BEING CURLED, SPRAYED, MASCARAED, AND LIPSTICKED, Bianca produced a dress from the black bag, and that's when River knew her sister had lost her ever-loving mind.

"There is no way I am wearing that," she laughed.

Bianca looked at the dress and back at River. "It's designer, and I got it for fifty percent off."

"How about I give you the other fifty percent, and you get me a whole dress?"

Bianca pouted. "You are going to be amazing in it. I got it for you. Please? Please? Please? Please?"

River took the long red dress cut low in the front. The slits in the legs almost met the v-neckline. She turned it around to find the back cut equally as low.

Of course.

"So, how am I supposed to keep this thing on my body?" she asked.

Bianca held up a small box of Scotch tape.

River stared at the dress again and shook her head. *Oh, what the hell?*

CHAPTER THREE

RIVER

The chauffeur helped River and Bianca from the back of the town car. River had never been in a car with a driver, not that she'd been much of anywhere in a car in her life. She'd never needed one while with her pack. She'd used her mom's Corolla only a few times when Cherry had sent her to town for supplies. Since she was in NYC, she did not want to go anywhere she couldn't get to by walking or bus. She rarely even used her motorcycle.

But a paid driver who got out and opened the door for her? Nope. Never.

Bianca squeezed River's bare arm as River took in the posh restaurant with a line down the block.

"Isn't it amazing?" Bianca asked. "I never thought I would mate someone so well off."

"You aren't faking it for his money, are you?"

Bianca stared in disbelief, and tears sprang to her eyes.

River patted her. "I'm kidding. Calm down. Your dad has enough money to give you whatever you asked for."

Bianca gave her a nervous smile and swiped at her eyes. "Oh, okay."

River's wolf grumbled at the jest.

So it wasn't the best joke, sue me.

River tended to say things without thinking them through sometimes.

"Dad would give you whatever you want too. He loves you as much as he loves me."

River's throat dried. She knew all too well how much Strider loved her. He'd been the one to pay for everything since she moved to New York. She had no idea how she would repay him. Not that he would ever ask.

River put on her best smile. "Let me meet this guy and ensure he's enough for my baby sister."

The smile returned to Bianca's face, and she pulled River toward the front door. "You're going to love him."

River checked to make sure her senses were locked down as they mixed with the multitude of humans. The smells of New York weren't something she thought she'd ever get used to. Plus, every once in a while over the last four years, she'd caught a whiff of something like honey and amber, and every time she did, panic seized her. So, she rarely let her senses go full bore unless she was too tired or preoccupied to notice.

Bianca marched up to the maître d' and smiled. "Hi. My uh... fiancé made a reservation today?"

The maître d' smiled politely. "I'm sorry, that's not possible.

We've been booked for three months. And as you see from the line, the waitlist is quite extensive."

Bianca pulled out her phone and showed it to the man. "But this is where he told us to come."

The maître d's smile tightened. "He must have been mistaken, Miss. As I said, we are booked out three months. There is no way-"

"Can you read the list?" River said.

The man turned his eyes on River, and the kindness of his smile began to crack. "I can read the list, but I assure you, if the reservations were made today, they were not at this restaurant."

"Maybe I should call him," said Bianca.

"And maybe he should do his job and read the reservation book."

The man's smile fell as he glared at River, but she couldn't care less. River could not abide by rudeness, especially toward her sweet little sister. Ever since Bianca and Strider came into her life River had protected Bianca like her own child. And just because they hadn't seen each other much in the past few years didn't change her instincts.

"What is the name?" the man asked tensely.

"Ezekiel Redmane," Bianca replied, typing away on her phone.

The man scanned his list and sniffed. "Sorry. No Redmane." His gaze landed on River, and she wanted to punch the smug smile off his flat face.

"Problem?" asked a handsome older man in an impeccable suit.

River and Bianca turned to the distinguished older gentleman. He inhaled deeply and smiled.

"Ah, Mrs. Redmane?"

"Uh… yes?"

He held his hand out to her and kissed the back of Bianca's

hand. "Zeke told me to expect you. He's expecting you and your sister. Please follow me." He opened a door and held it for them.

The Maître d' gaped at him. "But, there's no reservation."

The man nodded. "Her fiancé and his boss are personal friends of mine, Ricardo. They made the reservation with me. Come, ladies; you're in my private dining room."

Ricardo's mouth fell open, and River couldn't help but throw him a sardonic smile. "Have a pleasant night, Dic-ardo."

His cheeks reddened, and before he could say anything, River followed Bianca and the owner to the back of the restaurant.

River let her senses sharpen, taking in the restaurant's sights, sounds, and scents.

Mmmmmm... Filet Mignon.

RIVER TOOK LESS THAN A MINUTE TO REALIZE BIANCA WAS NOT after Zeke for his money. Tall and broad, he was boyishly handsome with blond hair and blue eyes. When they entered, Zeke immediately moved from his friend, and like a heat-seeking missile, he zeroed in on Bianca, pulling her into a passionate kiss.

A minute passed, and then another with the two locked together, and Zeke's hands began to roam areas better explored in private.

River cleared her throat. The two ignored her- if they even heard her.

"Zeke," the man at the table called. "Let her breathe. I thought we came here to eat, not witness you two get it on."

Bianca giggled, and Zeke reluctantly pulled his lips from hers.

"I missed you," he whispered.

Bianca kissed him again. "I missed you more."

Zeke growled. "Not possible."

The man at the table rolled his eyes and smiled at River. "Disgusting, isn't it?"

"I can't wait until you find your mate, Lachlan. I'm gonna totally let you have it." Zeke unwrapped his arms from Bianca and settled for taking her hand instead. He turned to River as Bianca wiped at her mouth and adjusted her dress.

"Zeke. I want you to meet my sister, River."

River stuck out her hand and shook with Zeke.

"It's a pleasure to meet you. Bianca has told me so much about you." He shook her hand, and a quizzical expression crossed his features. A chill swept through River, but the expression fell, and he smiled again.

So he wasn't an Alpha. Thank heavens. She wasn't sure Bianca was cut out to be a Luna.

River forced a smile. "I'd be interested in knowing what my sister told you."

Zeke chuckled. "Only good things."

River cocked an eyebrow at Bianca. "So, she's lied to you."

Bianca laughed and took River's arm. "Oh, stop. You're always too hard on yourself. You're amazing."

River nodded but didn't say anything.

"Bianca, River, this is my friend Lachlan. We work together."

"Friend?" Lachlan stood and smiled. "Wow. I'm so honored. You've never called me friend before."

Zeke shook his head. "Don't let it go to your head."

Lachlan snorted and took River's hand. He sniffed the air for a moment and glanced around. "Dang. What's that smell? Is it chocolate?"

"Nah, I think it's spumoni," Zeke replied.

"What's spumoni?" Lachlan pulled his hand back.

"It's like a pistachio cherry kind of ice cream."

Lachlan smiled. "Yum. I totally want some."

Lachlan didn't offer his hand to Bianca. Instead, he inclined his head to her.

Weird. Maybe in their packs, they did things differently. Shifters protected their mates, but she'd never known them to have a no-touch policy. But Bianca had said she'd left the area to go to the gathering. She needed to remember to ask Bianca where she'd gone.

Lachlan and Zeke led them to the table and pulled out their chairs. Suddenly, River got the sinking feeling Bianca had tried to set her up on a blind date.

River groaned inwardly and ordered a glass of wine.

Bianca chatted enough for all four of them over the next hour. After three courses, even River, with her healthy appetite, felt sluggish. Zeke remained as attentive as every male River had seen with their mate. He looked only at Bianca. Doting on her every want and need. Did she need her bread buttered? He did it. Pepper on her salad? How dare she lift a finger to grind it? He stopped short of cutting her food and feeding it to her, but not by much. Feeding one's mate was the most significant way a male could tell his female he would always protect and provide for her.

"So, where are you from?" River asked.

"I'm from Vermont," said Zeke.

River sipped her wine. "And what do you guys do?"

"Security," Lachlan replied.

River nodded. Not many shifters needed security details, but shifters made excellent security for humans. Their heightened senses made them the ideal bodyguards.

"What about you?" asked Lachlan. "What do you do, River?"

"River's an artist," Bianca said. "She's amazing. Her sculptures are to die for. She got her own show this weekend."

"You're coming, aren't you?" River asked.

Bianca nodded vigorously. "Of course. I would never miss it. I can't wait for people to oooohhh and aaaaahhhh over your talent."

River's cheeks heated. "I wouldn't go that far."

"I would! Especially the one in your workshop. It's exquisite! The way you-"

"Okay. Okay." River shook her head. "Enough. It's not the statue of David."

Bianca's eyes shone, and Zeke kissed the back of her hand.

The owner arrived and asked if they wanted dessert. They ordered spumonis all around with cups of coffee.

River ordered a second cup of coffee for Bianca. The guys didn't know Bianca as well as River did, and holding her liquor wasn't something Bianca did well. Her wolf genes helped her metabolize it quicker, but not as quick as most shifters, strangely. And River didn't want Bianca's new mate to think badly of her.

Dessert arrived, and the group ate and sipped the dark brew.

"What do you want to do now?" Lachlan asked.

With how much River had eaten, she only wanted to go to her place, curl up in bed, and sleep. But her wolf wanted to be out of the workshop for a while. And honestly, she was having a good time. There wasn't going to be a love match between her and Lachlan. Didn't matter, though, he was funny and sweet, and as far as blind dates went, he was the best one she'd ever had. The only one she'd ever had, but still. And who knew, perhaps they could be friends with benefits if she did things right.

"I know a club," River offered.

"A club?" Bianca practically jumped out of her seat. "Yes. Totally yes. I want to go dancing. I haven't been dancing in forever."

"Okay," Zeke chuckled. "Let's do it. We have time before we have to be back."

Zeke tried to pay the bill, but the owner refused his money and called their driver.

They all piled into the sedan, and River gave him the club's name.

When they arrived, the driver opened the door and helped the women from the back seat. The line to get into the club stretched down the street. River sauntered to the red velvet rope separating the humans from the shifters.

The bouncer spotted River and nodded. "Hey Riv. It's pretty full right now. You're gonna have to wait a few minutes."

River smiled, but Zeke stepped up to the immense gorilla shifter. "Is there a VIP section?"

Frank snorted. "Yup. But it's for VIPs. Sorry."

Zeke pulled a card from his pocket and handed it to Frank. Frank's eyes widened, and he undid the red rope.

"Right this way, Mr. Redmane."

How much money did Zeke have?

Lachlan placed a hand on River's back to usher her inside. Her wolf awakened but didn't move.

Frank winked at her as she passed. "You finish the wolf piece yet?"

She nodded. "I did tonight."

"Congrats. I've missed seeing you these last few months." He whispered. "You look amazing in that dress."

River blushed. Frank was a fantastic guy. If she'd been into interspecies mingling, she wouldn't have minded giving Frank a go.

Since living in the city, this was the only club she'd ever been to. It mainly catered to shifters, though humans were allowed as well. She'd felt more at home in the club than anywhere else in the city, so she'd come about once a month to dance alone and relax.

"You let me know if you have any problems. Don't want any males getting handsy with ya."

River patted Frank's bulky arm. "You never do."

Frank chuffed. "Damn straight."

Frank didn't know River's whole story, but he knew enough. She lived in the city because she was hiding. A lot of shifters were.

After her wolf had awakened, no amount of suppression pills on the planet would knock her out again. And as weeks had turned to months in the city and her wolf hadn't been allowed the opportunity to stretch, River had to find an alternative.

She'd scoped out the club for weeks before going inside for the first time. Slowly, little by little, she'd trained herself and her wolf not to become overwhelmed and freak out. As a matter of fact, after six months, her wolf had craved the weekly five-hour dance jam. Being able to move and dance amongst other shifters soothed her wolf.

Soon, it became the only place River would go and feel safe outside her apartment and the gallery. She learned every exit, even the secret ones. She knew every employee, and she memorized every foot of the floor, bar, and VIP room.

The lights and music struck River almost as hard as the overload of scents. A ripple coursed over River's skin and settled in her stomach.

Okay, girl, okay. Let's settle in, and I'll let you dance.

River peeled back her safeguards as they walked amongst the throng of shifters and humans. Too long. It had been too long since she'd released her wolf. She'd been so preoccupied with her work she'd neglected her other half.

Her wolf sniffed everything, taking it in.

I'm sorry, girl. I promise. I'll do better.

Clubbing was the only time her wolf didn't freak out in a crowd, being overly cautious. Just the occasional smell on the streets of New York could send her wolf into a panic. River couldn't blame her. They both still bore the scars of what had happened to them.

Tonight, she would let her wolf dance as much as she wanted.

RIVER LET THE MUSIC FLOW THROUGH HER AS SHE DANCED ACROSS from Bianca, Zeke, and Lachlan. She wasn't sure how she did it, or if everyone could, but she'd let down the barrier between her conscious self and her wolf and let her wolf guide her sometimes frenzied and erratic movements.

Five drinks had her relaxed, but due to her extra fast metabolism, it wouldn't last more than an hour at most. She'd never been a heavy drinker. She'd always been too controlling. Plus, she did not see the appeal of vomiting or embarrassing herself. She knew how much took the edge off without going into the out-of-control zone. And that's what she'd wanted from the night, to take the edge off and let loose.

Bianca, on the other hand, had a few too many flutes of champagne as she celebrated with Zeke. Like always, River felt responsible for watching after her sister, even with Zeke and Lachlan present.

As the song ended and the next one started, Zeke pulled his phone from his pocket and stopped dancing to read it. He said something to Bianca; she nodded, and he stalked off the floor, his expression serious.

River turned to Lachlan, who pulled his phone out before motioning River to the VIP area.

River nodded, and Lachlan started texting before he'd left the floor. What was that about? She scanned for Bianca. A second of panic coursed through her when Bianca wasn't where she'd left her moments earlier.

"Riviiieeeeeee-" Bianca called. "Come meet my new friends!"

Dammit. River had taken her eyes off Bianca for less than thirty seconds, and already the leggy brunette had two rogues grinding up on her. River stormed over and shoved the first male.

"Back off," she commanded, baring her teeth.

His eyes widened, and he backed away. Guy number two wasn't giving up so easily, though. He reached for Bianca's rear, and River twisted his wrist until his knees buckled.

"She's taken," she said through clenched teeth.

He swung at River with his free hand. Too bad for him Cherry had been exceptional at teaching River to fight.

River planted the pointy heel of her shoe on the inside of his thigh, right over the artery, and pressed down.

His swing stopped midair as he gripped her other leg.

"I said, she's taken, asshole." River moved her heel from his leg to his balls, and the guy let go of her. "Learn some respect before you're killed, idiot." She kicked him, and he doubled over. River let go of his arm, and he fell to the floor in a heap.

When she straightened, several of the encroaching males moved away.

Damn. What a way to ruin a fun buzz.

She turned. Yet another male was already approaching Bianca.

River shook her head. It had always been that way with Bianca. If Zeke was smart, he'd mark Bianca in the VIP section.

"Bianca!" River retrieved her sister and glared at the male. He looked like he might protest for a moment, but she let the slit in her dress widen, and her hand went to the knife she had strapped on her thigh.

He spotted it and backed off.

"River, what's wrong?"

"You're mated, Bianca. You can't do this anymore."

Bianca's eyes widened. "I… I didn't think…"

"No. You didn't. But you need to B. This isn't like when we would sneak out. Zeke is your mate, and if he saw them touch you, you can bet most of these males would already be bleeding or dead."

Bianca whimpered.

River hated scaring her sister, but this was New York, not upstate Connecticut.

Bianca tossed her arms around River's neck and right out of the trajectory of another male who'd been aiming for her. "You're the best sister ever. You always save my ass."

"That's my job." River hugged her back and sniffed her. The alcohol had begun to loosen its grip, but not quick enough. "Why don't we sit for a few minutes, okay?"

Bianca nodded.

River helped her sister to a VIP section.

"I'm thirsty," said Bianca.

"I'll bring you some water."

"With vodka in it?"

River gave her a pointed look.

"Water," Bianca repeated.

River nodded.

The VIP bouncer Kraeger moved to the side and let them through.

"You need anything, River?" he asked.

She shook her head. "We're fine. Thanks."

Kraeger nodded and went back to patrolling the dance floor.

River walked past several smaller VIP sofas to the larger, more private area in the back. She sat Bianca on the sizable round couch where Lachlan and Zeke were talking. Zeke took a giant step over the glass table, separating them.

"What happened?" He sniffed her.

"Nothing," said Bianca. "River saved me."

Zeke turned to her, and his gaze fiery.

"Just some rogues," River said. "I dealt with them."

Zeke ran his fingers through his hair. "I should have known better than to bring her here. I need to get her somewhere secure."

"Cool down," said River. "You can't lock her up. She's not property. I understand you are upset. As soon as you bond with her, males will keep their distance. Until then, you can't keep her in a vault and not expect her to live her life."

Zeke shook his head. "You don't understand."

"No, I'm pretty sure I do." River crossed her legs, exposing one of the knives.

He glanced at it and then at River.

"Living is dangerous for an unmated female nowadays."

"You can't understand because-"

Lachlan's phone buzzed. "Vanessa says the Boss will be here in a minute."

Zeke nodded to Lachlan. "Stay with them."

Lachlan moved to their side of the couch and sat as far from

Bianca as possible. But his eyes raked over her with an edge of worry.

Damn, the guys were the strictest and most possessive males she'd ever met, especially for Betas.

River tapped Bianca's hand. "Don't move. I'll bring water."

Bianca nodded, her eyes not quite as glassy, but she still did not comprehend the reality of what might have happened to her.

River knew, though. River knew all too well what happened with desperate rogues.

River stood and followed Zeke toward the door.

He stopped. "Where are you going?"

"I'm getting water."

"You need to stay put."

River's gaze hardened. "No. I don't. I am not your mate. Your mate is back there in need of water."

Something flickered in Zeke's eyes. River couldn't quite place. Fear possibly? Or something else.

He blinked several times and then nodded. "Of course. Sorry."

Zeke headed into the crowd, and River walked to the exit, and Kraeger looked down at her. "Don't let my sister out without me. Only me."

His gaze moved to Zeke, and his eyes narrowed.

She touched his arm. "It's nothing like that. Just don't let her dance again, okay?"

He nodded, and River made her way toward the bar. She was not taking a chance with Bianca. Lachlan wasn't about to do whatever was necessary to keep Bianca in the VIP area, and River was sure if Bianca went out of the roped-off area, Zeke might kill everyone in the place when he returned.

River wove through the throng of bodies, trying not to stab the roaming hands and leering, hungry stares.

Her wolf snarled and snapped at them.

Easy girl. It's how it is here.

Don't. Like.

River nodded. She got it.

She squeezed up to the crowded bar and leaned on it.

She couldn't help but smirk when more than one male tried to catch her eye and stare her into submission.

Pup, you have no clue what I've been through or who I am.

Ultimately, her wolf stared at them until their expressions became confused, and they turned away.

One of the perks she'd found out about being an Omega. No one outranked her. No one she'd met anyway.

A sudden commotion erupted as a group of men surrounding a much larger figure moved people out of the way on the floor.

Sheesh. Rude much?

Wait. Was that Zeke? *Damn.* Who was his boss that he needed an army of bodyguards?

People parted for them on the dance floor, and phones snapped photos everywhere.

Who was it, Jason Momoa?

A leggy strawberry blonde, a foot taller than River, wiggled in beside River and raised her hand for the bartender. "Excuse me!"

River rolled her eyes. Jimmy was the best bartender. A hawk shifter, he saw everyone when they came to the bar, no matter how many people approached. He also remembered what order they came in.

River was tempted to push the woman out of the way, but sadly, the night had begun taking its toll, and she found herself too tired to start yet another fight.

The bartender's gaze traveled from his current customer to River. "River, whatcha havin'?" he yelled.

She held up two fingers. "Water. Thanks, Jimmy."

The strawberry blonde sniffed River. She looked like she'd come straight out of the movies with her light eyes, smattering of freckles, and ruby lips. The curves her black dress hugged were every wolf's desire. And River couldn't help the pang of jealousy. Sure, she had decent boobs and a decent rear, but only surgery would give her that kind of hourglass. The kind wolves went nuts for. The kind that told them their mate would bear them healthy cubs.

The woman sniffed at River, her disdain palpable.

River's wolf bared her teeth.

We are Omega. Her wolf reminded her. River was tempted to stare the woman into submission, but didn't have the energy.

Not tonight, girl. Tonight is Bianca's night. I will not embarrass her in front of Zeke and his boss. No matter how much I would love to introduce the female's perfect nose to the bar.

Jimmy brought over the waters for River and smiled. "Stay hydrated."

"Excuse me," said the female huffily. "I need to order some drinks, please."

"Thanks, Jimmy." River plucked a ten from inside her dress and stuffed it in Jimmy's tip glass.

He winked at River, and she walked away.

"Excuse me? Hello?"

River glanced over her shoulder.

Jimmy eyed the female, his smile gone. "It's not your turn."

River snickered and pushed back through the crowd, which had turned all their attention to the VIP section.

Sheesh.

She nudged a guy out of her way, but he didn't move. Kraeger spotted her and moved several people out of the way before helping her up the steps.

"Hang on a sec, we're trying to clear the other parties out," he said.

The few other shifters in the VIP area exited, almost making River spill her water.

"Oh my gosh, is it him?"

"I think it is."

"Did you get a photo?"

"Hell ya, I did."

She sidestepped at the last second.

"Sorry, but your friends want the area extra secure. You have the whole place to yourselves now."

River wanted to ask him what was going on, but Kraeger walked down the steps and told the crowd to go back to dancing or leave.

River headed toward the back of the VIP section, but suddenly, her wolf stood up and inhaled. River stopped. She sniffed again, praying not to smell honey and amber, but she didn't.

Calm down, girl. We're fine. Everything is fine.

She moved closer to the back of the room, but her wolf became more agitated, and the hairs stood up all over her body. What the hell?

Bianca and Zeke came into view with half a dozen other men. She approached, and a man wearing an identical suit to Zeke's held his hand up to her.

"Sorry, private party."

She tried pointing with the glasses of water. "Yeah, that's my... Zeke!"

Zeke turned and pinned her with a look she couldn't back down from.

"I told you I went for water," she said.

He nodded, but his jaw worked hard. "My boss is in the bathroom. He'll be back in a minute. I don't want him to meet Bianca like this. I didn't realize she-"

"She doesn't," River blurted. "She doesn't drink. That's why this hit her so hard. I promise."

Zeke nodded, but his eyes darted over the other males near Bianca.

"I'll take her out of here," said River.

Zeke walked back to Bianca. She flung her arms around him again and kissed him hard. The other men, all wearing similar dark suits, looked away.

River's wolf whined.

River took a cleansing breath. What was with her? She looked at each male in turn as she walked to Bianca.

"Come on, B. Down this water, and you can go to my place to sleep until Zeke is done."

"But I want to stay with Zeke."

Zeke kissed and nipped Bianca's neck. For a second, River thought he'd marked her, but when he pulled away, the bite hadn't broken the skin. A memory threatened to bubble to the surface, but River shoved it down.

No way. Not now. She did not have time to relive that hell. Besides, Zeke wouldn't bite Bianca without her permission. He wasn't like that. He was too in control to lose it like a rogue would.

"Me too, babe," Zeke said. "But I have to work now. I explained this to you. Work has to come first."

Bianca frowned but nodded.

River took one of the glasses of water and gave it to Bianca.

She chugged it, and River handed her the second glass. She downed that one, and her eyes lost their glazed sheen.

Someone bumped River from behind, and she surged forward on her heels. Lachlan caught River's arm and glared behind her.

"Vanessa, don't be a bitch." Lachlan turned to her. "Are you okay?"

The entitled bitch from the bar sat on the sofa, her eyes pointedly focused on anyone but River.

"Don't mind her," Lachlan said. "She's a total asshole because… well, I have no idea why."

River and Lachlan laughed, but his smile fell as he looked over her shoulder. Everyone in the VIP room bowed their heads except Vanessa, who got to her feet and moved forward.

A strange chill swept through River, which morphed into an icy heat that made her skin flush. A strange sense of comfort washed over her like someone had wrapped her in a thick old quilt.

But as quick as the comfort came, a low growl sounded behind River, and she jerked to her senses again. Everyone's eyes were on her. No, not her… at someone behind her.

River spun around to find a massive male standing inches away.

Her wolf chuffed and backed up, pawing at the ground.

Up, and up, and up, River looked until she spotted the stubble gracing his chiseled jaw. An amazing scent surrounded her. She couldn't move her legs or think.

Her wolf went from zero to one hundred so fast River couldn't process what he looked like, what he wore, or anything else about him except that he was ginormous. Her wolf growled, chuffed, and then barked, confused.

What the hell?

River couldn't move. Couldn't breathe. Couldn't think. She swallowed hard and searched for Bianca's hand, but couldn't find it.

A rumble sounded in the male's chest, but River refused to meet his eyes.

What the hell was happening? She didn't know, but she didn't want to either. Something was off with her wolf. The last time something had been off, she hadn't listened to her wolf; she'd hesitated. She wasn't going to make the same mistake twice.

"It's time to go," she announced.

River turned and pulled Bianca from Zeke's arms, her wolf practically having a panic attack inside her.

What? What is it? River demanded. *What the hell is wrong with you?*

Her wolf's next word almost made River's heart stop beating. *Alpha!*

"Ares," a female voice called behind River. "Come on. There's a couch back here, and I ordered you a drink."

River's heart beat wildly. Away. She needed to get away. River hurried past several males who still hadn't moved from where they stood, heads bowed.

"Ouch. Sis, why are you dragging me?" Bianca asked.

Wait. Wait. Her wolf begged.

No!

River made it to the door of the VIP room before he spoke.

"Stop!" he commanded in a booming voice.

For the first time in her life, words stopped River in her tracks. River peered down at her feet and willed them to move, but they wouldn't.

What in the actual crap?

"Come back!" the Alpha demanded.

It took every fiber of River's will not to turn around and go back to him like a compliant little shifter. But somehow, she resisted the overwhelming pull his command had on her.

Zeke growled. "That's my mate."

River took the momentary distraction and reached for the door handle, but the male roared, and she froze again.

"Not her," he said. "You. Female. Come back!" His deep, booming voice held a note of threat and something else. Something soft like a caress down her spine. A need so visceral she almost wanted to obey him. Almost.

Go back! Go to him!

You've got to be kidding me.

Need. We. Need. Him.

A chill swept through River. *No. No. No.*

River's mind whirled, and the scents of the room filled her. *Males. Shifter males. Chocolate. Coffee. Leather. Whiskey. Gunpowder. Metal. Woods.* The scents mixed in a cacophony, like walking into a lotion store. But a heady aroma she recognized sent a chill up her spine.

Lycans. All Lycans.

Her wolf roared, and River yanked the door open. How had she not noticed? How had she missed it?

She took one step, and in the span of a breath, someone rushed past her, and where only a second before there had been an open door to the rest of the club, a giant white dress shirt wall stood in her way.

Not even her old Alpha could move that fast. She groaned as the most delicious fragrance enveloped her. Earth and woods mixed with vanilla and smoke, like a campfire-roasted marshmallow melting on the ground.

River's hands began to shake as she recognized small objects in front of her eyes as shirt buttons.

River's heartbeat thundered like a bass drum, but her wolf went silent.

Every sound fell away, and every other scent disappeared as she breathed in. A thick black leather belt rested less than a foot below her eyeline. And under the belt stood a solid pair of tree trunk-sized legs. Expensive fabric filled her eyes as she took in the weave of his shirt to the collar, which splayed open by two buttons. The sleeves had been folded to the elbows, exposing dark hair over tanned, muscular forearms.

She wanted to trace her fingers up his skin to his soft-looking hair.

Her wolf mewled. Actually frickin' mewled.

River shook. Between the Lycan's aura and her wolf, she fought to control herself.

"Look at me," he commanded.

She willed herself not to, but her wolf won out and propelled her eyes upward. Up and up to the broadest shoulders she'd ever seen. Then to a stubbly chin and finally a pair of bright blue-green eyes.

The moment her gaze locked on his, she flooded with desire, and her wolf howled.

Mate!

Without thinking, River raised her hand to stroke his chiseled but perfect face. All heavy angles crafted with master precision. She couldn't have shaped his face more perfectly out of marble if she'd spent her entire life working on it.

His gaze bore into her, making her legs wobble and her skin flush. Again, another jolt of heat traveled through her, followed by the comfort of a downy blanket.

Mine!

His massive hands wrapped easily around her waist. He turned his head and sniffed her hand. A growl rumbled in his chest, and he bent down and smelled her hair and face. Waves of Alpha aura floated off him, making her want to submit to him. Submit to his command. His desires. His touch. Even her wolf fell on her side, belly exposed to him.

Every millimeter of her wanted to rub against him. To explore him. To lick every plane of his massive body and commit it to memory.

River ran her fingers through his shaggy curls and breathed in his shampoo. Warmth shot through her, and desire pooled between her legs. When he sniffed her neck, she snapped back to reality. His lips grazed her skin, making her arms pebble. Memories flashed back of the attack, and she had to bury the scream that bubbled in her throat. Her legs refused to move, and her wolf remained in a state of submission.

Not again. She couldn't go through it again. Mentally, she checked her body, remembering where she'd concealed her knife. She reached for it, and he knelt, sniffing down her belly. When he looked up at her, his eyes were bright yellow. His fangs descended in his mouth down past his chin, and he lay his head on her breast.

"My Omega," he growled.

Her wolf mewled. *My Alpha.*

A rush of need washed over River like jumping into a hot tub. Her most private parts slicked, and a moan formed in her mouth.

Her body shook, and she wanted nothing more than to shove him to the floor and bury her fangs in his neck as he plowed into her.

Her fangs descended, and the need to bite him overtook all sense of reason.

Stop! She screamed at her wolf. *Back the F- down!*

But her wolf didn't listen. She rolled on her back submissively, not to River, but to the Lycan.

The Lycan dipped his head to her belly again and inhaled deeply before purring so loudly it vibrated River's body. The sensation soothed her again and made her want to push his face down further and have him-

No. No. No. No. This was not happening.

The world came crashing back down around her.

Music blared in her ears, and the odor of bodies and alcohol permeated her nose once more. She scanned his bodyguards frantically, who now knelt and bowed their heads to her. Except Vanessa, who gaped at the Lycan male like he'd lost his damn mind.

All she'd wanted was a night of possibly decent sex and to curl up in bed and fall asleep. Instead, she had a massive Lycan proclaiming her as his. Again. Only not so violently this time. And this time, her wolf agreed.

She looked to Bianca and Zeke for help. But heads bowed, they couldn't see her.

What the hell? Why were they acting like that?

Voices sounded outside the backroom, and all the men sprang to their feet. The Lycan moved her behind him, shielding her as all hell broke loose.

River didn't know the newcomers or how they'd gotten into the VIP room, but the Lycan in front of her roared and lashed out. He swung wildly, hitting one shifter after the next. Flashes of light blinded her as dozens of cameras clicked off. She couldn't take it. The rage. The violence. It all flooded back.

His fangs on her neck. His blood splashing her as she stabbed him. The look in his eyes as Cherry yanked him off her.

Zeke and the other bodyguards jumped on the Lycan Alpha to restrain him. Vanessa shoved River out of the way.

Terrified, River clutched Bianca's hand and dragged her backward. They banged into the rear wall, and a panel creaked behind her. River shoved it open to a secret passage and raced down it.

"River, stop. Where are we going?" Bianca asked.

But River didn't stop. Something inside her told her to run. Not her wolf, who howled in pain, but the other part of her. The human part. The part that wanted to continue with her simple life and not become a breeding bitch to a monster. A hot, ripped monster. But still, a monster.

They reached the end of the passage, and River shoved open a small door leading down to the alley. River raced down the steps with Bianca stumbling behind.

"River. Stop. Stop." Bianca pulled on her arm as they reached the sidewalk in front of the club. "I need to find Zeke."

River couldn't think.

Bite.

Couldn't breathe.

Blood.

She needed to run.

Stab. Stab. Stab.

Her wolf growled and snarled to be let out. To go back. To find him.

My Alpha.

River's soul cleaved in two as her wolf fought her for control.

She couldn't take it. She tore off her heels and handed them to Bianca.

"River, wait. Where are you going?" she called. "You have to go back. I think he's your mate."

Exactly.

River's claws extended, as did her fangs. She ripped the slit in her dress higher, turned, and ran.

It couldn't have happened. Not to her. Not again. She couldn't be his mate. It wasn't possible.

His beautiful eyes floated back into view, and River howled as she ran. Tears streamed down her cheeks.

Not again, she prayed to the Wolf Goddess. *Please don't mate me to a Lycan. Not again.*

ARES

"WHERE IS SHE?" ARES BELLOWED. "WHO IS SHE?"

"Ares, calm down." Vanessa reached for him.

He swatted her away and bared his teeth. "Don't touch me."

Zeke, Theo, and Santiago cleared the club of the press, breaking their equipment and buying the cellphones off every person before they left. Now, in the silence of the dead space filled with too many aromas for Ares to process, he fought to catch her scent again.

She'd run from him. All these years, he'd searched for his mate, thinking he would never find her, and upon their first meeting, she'd run. An Omega. The rarest of rare. The sacred above all.

"Zeke!" he yelled. "She was here with your new mate, wasn't she?"

Zeke nodded and moved swiftly to Bianca's side, putting a protective arm around her and pulling her to him.

"Who is she?" he demanded, looking between Zeke and his mate.

"She's my mate's sister… sort of," Zeke answered. "I mean, their parents have been together for a while-"

Bianca swatted at Zeke. "She's my sister."

Ares strode to them. "What is her name? Where can I find her?"

Zeke's eyes flashed. He wasn't an Alpha or a full Lycan. He was one of Ares' faithful hybrids. Even so, the message was clear: Ares had to calm down with Zeke's mate, or there would be a problem.

"Her name is River Whitetail," Zeke said, his voice strained.

River. The beautiful, petite, silvery-haired beauty who might break if he held her too close was named River. How she'd looked at him with her bright sapphire eyes had been like no one else in the world existed. At twenty-eight, he'd all but given up on finding his true mate, and he'd only ever fantasized about finding an Omega. So when he'd smelled her, it had literally brought him to his knees. His wolf paced and howled, ready to rip the city apart to find her.

Mine. My mate. Find. Mate. Bond.

Vanessa moved toward him again, but he pinned her with his gaze, her very presence irritating. "Go to the hotel," he commanded. "Prepare for my mate's arrival."

Shock registered on her face for a split second, then she bowed and complied. Vanessa was nothing more to him than a subordinate. She'd been his assistant for five years and occasionally shared his bed when he couldn't take the loneliness. But no more. Looking at her tempted him as much as looking at his men. Zero.

Vanessa passed him without a word, and as soon as she'd left, he glanced over his men who awaited his command.

Nothing mattered more than finding his mate. His Omega. She was in the city. Alone in the city. An Omega. How was it possible?

He'd heard the rumors one had been born, but he'd been too busy dealing with the rogue issues to see if the rumors were true.

But now... He'd been such an idiot. He should have been searching the whole time. And how had he not smelled her as soon as he'd entered the club? There were many people, shifters and humans alike, but he should have been able to smell her. To sense her, but he hadn't. Not at all.

Desensitizing spray? Since she was an Omega and a shifter. She probably used a desensitizing spray. It had to be because it had been a full two seconds after she'd bumped into him before he'd caught the whiff of her beautiful perfume. Of pistachios, vanilla, and sweet cherries, and he'd wanted nothing more than to bathe in her scent. But the moment their eyes had locked, she could have sprayed all the desensitizing spray in the world on herself, and he would have smelled her. When he'd laid his head on her breast, her perfume had intensified so much it had taken everything inside him to keep from ripping off her panties and burying his face in her most delicious parts.

But the stupid paparazzi had shown up and scared her off. His poor little wolf. He needed to find her. More than needed. He'd die if he didn't. He'd spare no expense. Rip down all of America to find her. Burn it building by building if he had to. No matter what it took.

"Where does she live?" he asked.

Bianca gave him an address, and he nodded, trying to keep his wolf from running all the way there.

"Take me to her." It wasn't a request.

Zeke looked to Lachlan. Lachlan nodded and exited.

Ares paced, his slacks painfully restraining his erection. His skin itched, and his wolf clawed at his insides to be let out.

Find her. Mark her. Ours.

"Your Majesty," Theo said. "May I suggest a drink?"

"Do you think I want a drink?" Ares snarled.

"No," Theo said calmly. "But all things considered, it might help. Believe me, I know how you feel right now-"

"When you found Micah, did she flee from you?"

Theo didn't answer.

Ares couldn't stop himself from being an Alpha-hole. Every inch of his body burned for her. To hold her. Kiss her skin. To take her back to his estate and lock her away from the terrible world.

"I'm sorry," Ares drove his hands into his hair.

Theo was Ares' oldest friend and closer than any twin brother.

Theo signaled the others to prepare to leave before approaching Ares and laying his hands on Ares' shoulders. "Trust me. We will find your mate, River Whitetail."

Ares looked from Theo to his other men. "Is this how all of you feel when you are away from your mates?"

The men nodded.

Only two of his men were born Lycans like Ares himself. Brothers Theo and Santiago. The other hybrids he'd turned a few years back. Even so, the one thing the hybrids had told him was the bonds to their mates were as strong and fierce as any Lycan's to a mate- except for an Alpha to an Omega. That bond... no one understood. Just like no one understood how the moon circled the earth day in and day out without stopping or getting tired.

Alphas and Omegas were fated. Destined for each other in a

way no other mated pair was. They were the embodiment of the Moon Goddess and her love, the Wolf God made flesh.

"I'm an asshole. I had no idea. Forgive me," Ares said.

The men told him he needn't apologize, but Ares shook his head.

"No. I won't have this for you. You've all been loyal and true. Tomorrow morning, you will each prepare your mates to come live on the estate so you can be closer and so they can have each other for support when you are working. Besides, there's nowhere safer. Especially now. I'm sorry it took so long to realize how much you need them. I'm sorry I've put myself above your bond and your needs. It won't happen anymore."

His men bowed. "Thank you, Highness."

Lachlan entered. "Got the car, Boss."

Ares nodded and stalked to the exit. "Let's go."

CHAPTER FOUR

RIVER

River raced back to her studio. She'd stripped off her dress from the club, yanked on jeans and a T-shirt, and slung on her backpack before jumping on her motorcycle and tearing off into the night.

My Omega.

The words echoed in her head. No. No way. She wasn't someone else's; she was her own. She fought to keep the memories of being attacked out of her head. At least this time, the male hadn't bitten her without permission. If he had, she would have stabbed his ass like the last one.

As she sped down the streets, weaving in and out of lanes of traffic, she couldn't get him out of her head. His scent. His eyes. His touch. Even as her mind screamed for her to get away, her wolf cried for her to go back. And the way her body had responded… had been embarrassing.

But she couldn't- he was a Lycan. A terrorizing, narcissistic, shifter-shredding, overbearing, animalistic killing machine. She wasn't stupid. She may not have paid tons of attention to all the folklore of pack meetings, but she had listened to the stories of one thing: the Lycans.

The original race of werewolves was stronger, faster, and less human than any other shifter species. They ruled the shifters from their home in Montreal and rarely came to the States except for business. They were the boogeymen mothers warned their pups about.

"You better behave, or the Lycans will come for you."

Like some kind of nightmarish Santas who saw you when you slept and knew when you were naughty.

River hit the 78 and continued east. She may not know what she was doing, but she knew where she planned on going. She wouldn't be safe for long, but she didn't need long, just enough time to clear her head and figure a way out of the mess the Wolf Goddess had dunked her in. Again.

River stopped her bike outside the small, faded cornflower blue house with dirty white shutters. The lights remained off inside- not that she'd expected them to be on; no one had been there in at least a decade.

She walked her bike up the drive and parked it in the detached garage next to her mom's old bike, then she walked to the back door and opened it. The familiar fragrance of lemon and pine cleaner mixed in the stale air filled her with a dozen emotions: sadness, longing, loneliness, and comfort. She stood in the kitchen and shut her eyes, remembering her dad's voice, the aroma of his chocolate chip pancakes, and the glow of their old television as they'd watched cartoons together.

Her ribcage tightened, and she imagined what her father would think of her latest 'stunt' as her mother would call them.

She dropped her bag on the kitchen table before weaving through the never-changing decor. She walked down the hall to the first bedroom and dialed in the code to the padlock she left to keep people out. They may not lock their doors in her old pack, but that didn't mean she wanted people pillaging her personal space. Not that they would. Those who knew her mother knew better than to mess with her.

She removed the padlock and opened the door to the small but brightly colored room. Before she found her muse in sculpting, she'd started with drawing and painting. And when she'd tired of using paper, she'd moved on to the walls and her furniture.

"It's yours, do what you want with it," her mom had said.

So, she had.

River breathed a sigh and locked the padlock inside the door. She'd never done that before, but back in her childhood home, surrounded by nothing but her memories, the extra security would comfort her as she slept.

ARES

ARES STROLLED THROUGH THE SPACIOUS WORKSHOP, TOUCHING various objects and inspecting the surfaces. He walked to a makeshift shower in the corner and lifted a discarded shirt from the floor. He held it to his nose and breathed it in. His wolf howled at her scent. The aroma of metal and oil mixed with pistachio and vanilla. His body sprang to life, and he had to adjust himself to keep his painful erection from bursting through his suit pants.

"Where is she?"

"I... I don't know, Y-Your Majesty," Zeke's mate stammered. "This... this is her place. Her only place. She doesn't have anywhere else."

He balled up the shirt and shoved it inside his coat. "Where's her apartment?"

"Upstairs." The female pointed.

Ares leapt the stairs and opened the door to the studio apartment. Her fragrance almost brought him to his knees as it saturated every surface.

The neat, orderly studio apartment stood in stark contrast to the workspace below. It'd been furnished with brightly colored furniture and paintings, but somehow, it all went together.

He walked to the bed area and took in the plush faux fur blanket. His wolf growled as he imagined how many men had been with her in the bed. The thought that someone else may have touched her body made him want to rip the bed to pieces and burn it. He walked to a small wooden nightstand and picked up the book she had. A romance called Red the Were Hunter. He turned it over and noticed a stack of other shifter romance books on the floor. Promised at the Moon, Cursed by the Moon, a dozen or so more. He shook his head and placed the book back on the nightstand.

He opened the drawer, and his fangs descended into his mouth as he picked up the small battery-operated toy, which smelled like the most intimate parts of her. He ran his hand over the soft silicone and imagined her alone in bed, naked and-

"Majesty," Zeke said behind him.

Ares shoved the purple toy back into the drawer and slammed it shut. "What?'

"My mate says River's motorcycle is gone."

Ares clutched the edge of her bed, and his fingernails lengthened, puncturing the furry pink blanket and the mattress beneath.

His body shook as his wolf surfaced, and he howled into the air.

Where is she?

"Bring your mate up here," he ordered.

Zeke growled, and Ares looked at him.

"Please. I only want to ask her some questions."

"I won't leave her alone with you."

"I didn't ask you to."

Zeke looked like he might say something else. Instead, he walked out and returned a minute later with his sultry but terrified-looking mate locked in his grasp.

Ares fought to keep his voice calm and forced his best smile onto his face.

"What is your first name, Mrs. Redmane?"

"Bianca, Majesty."

Ares looked to Zeke. "May I call her by her first name?"

Zeke nodded once, but Ares didn't miss his tense posture nor the fact that he kept his arms wrapped protectively around her. The rules weren't clearly defined regarding his position regarding his men's mates. His men became part of his pack, but technically, they'd never discussed whether their mates would be part of it. Except for Theo, none of the others had taken Lycans as mates.

"Bianca, where would River go if she wanted to get away?"

"I… I don't know, Majesty." Her eyes rounded fearfully.

"Where is her pack?"

Bianca's eyebrows scrunched together. "Mom and Dad relocated years ago to Andover. But she wouldn't go home."

"Why?"

"Because she and our mom don't... they aren't close. And... she has bad memories from Andover. She hasn't been back in four years."

"Where would she go?" he asked, trying to keep his voice passive.

Bianca shook her head.

"Tell Lachlan we are going to Andover."

Zeke nodded and turned with Bianca to leave, but Bianca turned back.

"Your Majesty, if I might. River has an art exhibit this week. She wouldn't miss it for anything."

"An exhibit?"

She nodded. "For her sculptures. It's at the gallery where she works."

Bianca opened her purse, pulled out a cream and gold envelope, and handed it to him.

Ares ran his fingers over the embossed type and checked his watch. Over thirty-six hours until the showing. He didn't think he'd be able to wait without his wolf ripping through him and everything standing between them.

"Thank you," he said. "Let's check Andover first."

Zeke and Bianca walked out.

Ares rubbed the invitation as he gazed over the floor of River's studio. His eyes landed on an intricate metal sculpture of a wolf mid-jump. Was that what River looked like in wolf form?

We will know soon enough; he promised his wolf.

CHAPTER FIVE

RIVER

River awoke to a bang on her bedroom door. She bolted out of bed and grabbed the bat by her dresser. Her heart pounded as she anticipated the door bursting into splinters. Her grip tightened on the bat when another bang slammed her door.

"River! I know you're in there. Get up."

River let go of her bat as she sighed. It wasn't the Lycan- though all things considered, she wasn't sure if she wished it was him instead.

She walked to her door and undid the padlock.

Cherry stood naked in front of her, sweat beading on her skin.

"Nice to see you too, Mom."

"Don't give me that shit. What did you do?"

River shook her head. "What are you talking about?"

"You know damn well what I'm talking about."

The blood rushed from River's body to her toes. "He found you?"

"If you mean the Lycans, yeah, they found me. They came into town all high and mighty and looking for you. We told them we hadn't seen you in more than a year, and after sniffing around for an hour, they left, satisfied we weren't harboring you. So, what the hell happened? Did you forget your spray? Your pills? What?"

"Why do you think I did something?"

"Because Lycans wouldn't be looking for you if you hadn't."

River rubbed her forehead. "Can you please put some clothes on? You may not be big on modesty, but I've seen you naked enough to give me a permanent inferiority complex."

Her mom snorted and stalked down the hall to her bedroom.

River glanced in the mirror. She opened a drawer and pulled out a brush, trying to flatten the tangled mess of curls from the night before.

"Did you tell them where I am?" she called.

Her mom walked back in, pulling a tank top over her breasts. "I may be a shit mom, but I'm your shit mom, and I'm not going to hand you over to some Lycan assholes." She sat on River's bed. "I didn't let the last one take you, did I?"

River brushed her hair for a moment.

"Did you become lazy? Stop following our protocols?"

River rolled her eyes. "You must think I'm a dumbass."

"What then?"

She caught her mom's eye in the mirror. "Worse."

Her mother paled in a way River had only seen once before. Fear tainted the air.

"River, no."

"Yup."

She jumped to her feet and turned River around, looking over her with genuine concern. She moved River's hair and checked River's neck and breasts.

"Did he mark you?"

"No."

"Did he rape you?"

"No, mom. He didn't do anything to me except…"

"Except what?" Her mom searched her face.

"Called me his Omega and hugged me."

Confusion crossed her mom's face. "But he didn't take you? Mark you? Hurt you?"

She shook her head. "I ran. Hence the reason he is searching for me. He's Zeke's boss."

"Zeke? Bianca's soon to be mate?"

River nodded.

"How could Bianca be so stupid? Why would she introduce you?"

"Because you and Strider thought it was better she not know what happened to me. Zeke is a hybrid. His boss is an Alpha Lycan of some sort."

Her mom opened the closet and tossed a duffle bag into the room. She retrieved clothes River hadn't worn in ten years and piled them on the bag.

"Mom, what are you doing?"

"I'm getting you out. You can stay with your Uncle Jape in Alaska. It should be far enough away." Her mom pushed past her, opened her drawers, pulled out a handful of cotton underwear and socks, and shoved them into the bag.

"I need to buy you some winter stuff. No. I'll call Jape. I'll have him pick up stuff when you arrive."

"Mom-"

"I'll have to buy you a ticket, but it can't be in your name. You'll need a fake I.D. Strider can do it."

"Mom-"

Her mom ran from the room, and River followed her to her bedroom. Cherry pulled up the rug and removed several wooden planks, exposing the safe below.

"I have money I can give you, and you have your trust fund, but I'll need to figure out how to send you money without them finding out-"

"Cherry!" River shouted. "I'm not going to Alaska."

Her mom huffed. "The hell you aren't."

"No. I have an art show tomorrow night. I have to go. I've spent six months getting everything ready."

"River. What is more important? An art show or your life?"

She didn't answer.

"Now you are being a dumbass. Do you not remember what happened the last time an Alpha Lycan found you? This one will be no different. He will take you, enslave you, chew you up, and spit you out, River." Her mom stood and moved to her. "And I know you, River. You won't submit. You won't give in. You'll fight and fight and fight until one of two things happens. He breaks you, or he kills you. And I won't let that happen to any daughter of mine."

River's wolf whined.

No. He won't.

Nothing about the male's actions has suggested he meant her harm. She remembered the look in his eyes as he'd gazed at her. Like she was the only thing in the world. The way he'd touched her, sniffed her, protected her from the cameras.

"Maybe not all of them are like the stories."

Cherry snorted. "If you believed that, you wouldn't have come here."

Had she been scared of mating or scared of him?

"Okay," River said. "I'll go to Alaska. But I must at least stop by the gallery."

"River-"

"Mom, it may be the only chance I ever get. I've spent my whole life dreaming of this. I can't walk away and never know if I was good enough. I have to do it for Dad."

Her mom stared at her. "Okay. It will take about a day to organize your paperwork. What time is it?"

"Five."

"I'll find you a flight at eight from JFK. But you can't arrive any later than six thirty, or you won't make take-off."

"I understand."

Her mom tossed her the duffle bag, pulled a gun from the safe, and handed it to her.

"Stay here. Lock yourself in your room. There's food in the pantry. I'll have Strider come for you tomorrow to take you to the gallery and then to the airport."

"You're not taking me?" River didn't like how little her voice sounded.

"If they will be watching anyone, it will be me. I snuck out and got here by shifting in the woods and keeping to the back roads. But once I return, there's no telling where they are or who might be watching me."

They stood awkwardly before her mom reached out and tugged on the end of the River's remaining curls.

"You can do this. You're my daughter, after all."

River nodded as her throat tightened. She gripped the duffle bag harder to keep from reaching for her mom.

"Believe it or not, I do love you, River."

River nodded as tears flooded her eyes.

"We'll get through this. I promise. I won't let anything happen to you."

STRIDER ARRIVED TO PICK HER UP AT THREE THIRTY THE NEXT DAY. He produced a bag and a dress on a hanger.

"I brought you a few things I thought you might want to use for your big night. I don't know if they are helpful or not. They're Bianca's, so I figured they might be useful."

River smiled at him. "Thanks, Strider."

"And here." He held out Bianca's bright red prom dress. "It's all I found that was fancy."

"This is perfect," River lied.

He nodded. "I'll watch TV while I wait."

"Okay." She closed the door awkwardly. She loved Strider; he was a wonderful guy, but he just… wasn't her dad.

River tossed the prom dress onto her bed and dumped out everything in the bag.

She thumbed through the various makeup items, hair accessories, and nail polishes- as if she had time to paint her nails.

She scrutinized the red dress and picked out a matching red rose clip, mascara, and lipstick. Guess red was her color for the evening.

IT DIDN'T LOOK BAD AFTER RIVER REMOVED THE POUFY SLEEVES AND mermaid tail from the red dress. The sweetheart neckline made her boobs appear bigger, which was a plus, and the skintight dress showed off her svelte figure and slender arms.

She pinned her hair to the side and clipped the red rose behind her ear. A sweep of mascara and the bright lipstick made her ocean-blue eyes pop.

She inspected herself and realized it might be the last time she saw her old bedroom for a long time.

She went to the windowsill and wiggled the rotted wood board at the bottom. It popped off, revealing a small space in the wall. She stuck her arm to the bottom and retrieved a small tin box. She sat it on her lap, running her fingers over the vintage scene whose paint had chipped off years before.

A light knock on her door pulled her from her thoughts, and she shoved the tin box into the duffle bag with all her other stuff and went to the door.

She pulled it open, and Strider took her in.

"Wow," he said. "I like it."

"Thanks."

He took the bag, put his arm around her shoulders, and kissed her head.

"Come on, Kid, let's get you to the party and off to safety."

River leaned into his shoulder as they walked, and for a moment, she didn't miss her dad so much.

THEY PULLED UP IN FRONT OF THE ART GALLERY AT FIVE-O-FIVE. River sat in the car, scanning the area and watching the people inside milling about, looking at the artwork.

"I can take you straight to the airport if you want," Strider offered.

Part of her wanted to say yes, but she couldn't. She'd worked too hard for this moment and needed to see at least what people thought of her work.

"I'll be back." She opened the passenger door.

"I'll circle the block until you come out."

She turned and smiled at him. "Thanks, Strider, for… everything."

He gave her a lopsided grin. "You're my girl, River, just like Bianca. Always have been."

Her heart constricted, wishing she'd done more to let him in. She kissed his cheek and exited the old muscle car.

The busy street bustled around her as she stepped up on the curb and pulled open the glass door. Her boss's assistant, Tiffany, raced to her with a frantic expression.

"Oh my gosh, there you are. Andrea has been calling you for two days."

"I… lost my phone."

"Thank heavens we got to your studio and packed up your last piece. It's amazing, by the way. I'm so glad we could bring it here and get it up in less than six hours. You did want it here, didn't you?"

River patted Tiffany's arm. Tiffany always rambled when nervous, and she was ultra-nervous from the sound of it.

Tiffany linked her arm to River's. River's heartbeat so loud she was sure everyone in the room heard it. People drank champagne and snacked on canapes while looking at paintings by various new artists from around town.

"Come on, you must see your space. Andrea couldn't get your final approval on the placement of the pieces, and she's been having a total conniption fit over it. I told her it looked amazing, but she wouldn't believe me. Only you can reassure her." Tiffany dragged her into the back gallery.

River stopped, and her breath caught for a moment. The six best pieces she'd ever created were among the brick walls and antique wooden floor. People gathered around each one, pointing to various aspects and smiling.

River couldn't help but smile at the reactions.

Strings of Edison lights hung from the ceiling, adding a warm glow to the space and bouncing off the steel and iron sculptures. River took it all in for a moment, entranced by what she'd created.

"River!" Her boss's sharp, sultry tone brought her out of her reverie.

River blinked, and her boss bustled over, a smile plastered too brightly on her face.

"Here she is everyone. The artist and my own protégé River Whitetail."

Clapping and cheers erupted all over the room, making River's cheeks heat. She dropped her gaze to the floor, and the clapping died down. Andrea took her arm and showed her around, introducing her to more people than she could remember the names of. People oohed and ahhed at her work and craftsmanship. She thanked each in turn before being swept away to meet someone new.

"River," said Andrea. "I'd like for you to meet a dear friend of mine, Ed Simons. He's the director of the Metropolitan Museum of Art."

He bent his head and kissed the back of River's hand. "Charmed, my dear lady. Your work is quite remarkable."

River's throat dried so fast she couldn't form words.

"I told Andrea I would love to have one outside my house in my garden. We've redone our estate with a full garden in the back, complete with a hedge maze, and I think one of your sculptures would be the perfect surprise to stand in the center of the maze for my guests to discover."

"Well... I... I don't know what to say. I am so honored. Of course, these are all for sale, or if you want something different, I would be happy to make it for you."

Ed nodded. "The one of the wolf and the rabbit in the corner would be perfect, but Andrea has informed me it's sold."

River swallowed hard. "It is?"

Andrea nodded. "Yes. All of your pieces sold within sixty seconds of the doors opening."

"I... I don't understand. How? Who-"

"I bought them," a low voice boomed in her ear.

Shivers ran over River's body as a warm palm landed on the small of her back, and the delicious scent of smoke and vanilla filled her nostrils. Her wolf howled in delight, but River's heart sank. How had she not caught his scent when she'd walked through the door? Better yet, how had he found her? How had he known about the exhibit? It wasn't like they put up ads across Central Park or anything.

Andrea smiled at the man standing so close to River, his thighs pressed against hers from behind.

Heat wafted through her again at his nearness, and she fought the desire to turn and look at him. Damn, he smelled amazing, and as his thumb traced a circle on the small of her back, her body threatened to betray her.

Stop! Just Stop!

"River. This is the gentleman who has so amazingly bought your entire collection. All you have to do is agree to the price and sign the contract."

River thought she might faint as she faced those beautiful, intense green-blue eyes. His eyes softened as he took in her face, and she fought the need to rake her fingers through his soft hair again. Not that she would have been able to since he'd slicked it back. He had also shaved, revealing a stronger jawline than she'd thought.

"Excuse me for not introducing myself," he said. "My name is Prince Ares Wolvenguard of the Montreal Wolvenguards."

Prince. Prince? Did he say, Prince?

River's legs committed mutiny, and Ares slipped his arm around her waist, steadying her.

He chuckled. A warm, rumbly sound. "Seems I have caused the lady to swoon. I think she might need a moment. Can we use your office, Andrea?"

It wasn't so much a request as a statement. But the award-winning smile he aimed at Andrea made Flynn Rider's smolder look like nothing more than a toddler's puppy-dog eyes.

Andrea smiled. "Of course, Your Highness. When you are done talking price, I will witness the contract for you."

He shot Andrea a toothy smile, lighting up his face and making River's heart forget its job.

He gripped River's hip tightly as he escorted her out of the gallery and down a short hall to Andrea's office. The sensation sent waves of fear and desire coursing through her.

What the hell was wrong with her? Her body had a mind of its own. Heating and wanting to be touched, though it was beyond inappropriate. She'd never been a PDA kind of girl.

River scanned for an exit, but there wasn't any. He held the door for her as she stepped into the office before closing and locking it. No escaping him this time.

Within a heartbeat, he had her pinned to the cold brick wall, his hard body pressing against hers gently. Terror overtook her, and she once again couldn't make her legs work. She closed her eyes and waited for what he might do next. Would he yell at her? Strike her? Reject her?

His hot lips slid down her throat, and she involuntarily let out a moan.

"You ran from me," he growled into her skin.

He pinned her arms above her head, and her pulse kicked up as his palms wrapped around her skin.

"Did you realize what had happened between us?"

She nodded.

"And still, you ran from me." He searched her face. "Though you knew you were my mate."

Her wolf howled. *My Alpha. My Mate. Mine.*

The longer he pressed against her, the closer she came to giving in to the mating bond and letting him take her against the wall.

"Say something. I want to hear your voice."

"Something."

A slight smirk crossed his lips. "A smart-ass as well as a runner. Interesting."

River couldn't make her brain work. Every fiber of his body pulled on hers like a magnet, forcing her to focus on him and only him. She didn't like feeling so out of control.

He scoured her face as if committing it to memory in case she got away again.

"Please let go of me," she said.

He lowered his mouth to her neck again and placed a hot kiss on her skin. "Why?"

The sensation snapped River back to reality like a lightning jolt to the lady parts. She wriggled in his grasp as anger bubbled inside her.

"Because I asked you to." Her voice came out stronger than anticipated, and his head whipped up. "You do know about consent, right? You say you want to do something to me; I say no, you comply."

"But you're mine, Little Wolf. You can't say no to me."

River clenched her jaw. "I can, and I do. Now let me go before I scream bloody murder."

His gaze steeled. "I could have marked you the other night or the moment I got you in this room. As heir to the Lycan throne, there are few rules about what I can and cannot do."

Seriously? Shifter rules didn't apply to him? Human decency didn't apply either, presumably.

"Your point?" she asked, wrenching her wrists from his grasp.

He blew out a harsh breath and took a step back from her. "My point is, I didn't do those things. I didn't rip apart your pack and demand they find you for me. I waited. Hell knows it's the hardest thing I've ever endured, but I did. I waited for you to come out of the shadows."

"And what? I'm supposed to thank you for not being a monster?"

"Yes."

"Okay. Thank you for doing what any normal person would do, not being an asshole rapist like the last one."

He was back on her in a flash, teeth bared, eyes black as pitch, but to River's surprise, the sight didn't scare her like last time.

"What do you mean the last one?" His Alpha aura and rage flowed off him like molten lava.

River moved her hair to the side, revealing the ragged scar on the side of her throat.

A painful whine cut off the roar rumbling through him. "Who did that?" he demanded through clenched teeth.

She shrugged, but his eyes flashed. It wasn't the time to be flippant. She had to knock it off if she wanted to make it through the story without him destroying everything in the room.

"I don't know," she whispered. "A rogue. He showed up about four and a half years ago. He found me in the kitchen with the pack wives preparing a meal. He bit me without consent. Until then, I'd not known I was an Omega."

He watched her, his breath drawing in and out in sharp bursts. "What did you do?"

"Well, first, I stabbed his ass with a potato peeler about half a dozen times. Then my pack Alpha came in with his Betas, and they pulled him off me. My mom shot him, I slashed his face open, rejected him, and stabbed him again."

She couldn't tell if Ares wanted to kiss her or kill her from the deadly, confused gleam in his eyes.

"You rejected him," he repeated.

"Of course. My wolf screamed he wasn't the one. Plus, you heard the part where the asshole tore into me without permission, right? Yeah, I'm kind of funny about things like that."

His eye twitched, and he swallowed hard. "And what does your wolf say about me?" His voice came out gentler than she'd expected it.

"She hasn't made up her mind yet."

A low chuckle escaped him. He took in her face for a moment and then sniffed her. "Doesn't smell that way to me, Little Wolf."

"It's the stupid mating bond, only, trust me," she lied.

He bent in until his mouth brushed hers. "Is it?"

Her breathing hitched as he ran his tongue over the seam of her lips.

"I taste you, Little Wolf. Your words may deny me, but the rest of you can't lie. Your wolf is telling you the same thing mine is telling me. We belong together. The chemistry between fated mates is too sacred for anything to cover it up. And once we are mated, nothing will keep us apart."

Without warning, he slammed his lips onto hers, and for a split second, River's body exploded, and even her wolf howled for him to take her. But as his tongue claimed her mouth, she turned her head away, breaking the kiss.

He groaned, and she turned back to him defiantly.

He traced one hand up her thigh and under her dress, grabbing her hip.

She bit her cheek until blood welled on her tongue.

"I will not take you today, River Whitetail, though it is both my right and my overwhelming desire. But I tell you now, before long, you will be my mate, and you will beg me to take you."

"They will chew you up and spit you out, River."

She smiled. "And I assure you, Prince Ares Wolvenguard, I will not."

A cocky smirk crossed his lips, and his eyes faded back to their mesmerizing bluish-green.

"We shall see, my beloved. We shall see."

CHAPTER SIX

ARES

It took Ares every ounce of control he possessed to keep by River's side without having his hands running over every creamy section of her body or wanting to throw a sheet over her, so no one saw the perfect skin made for him.

Only the sight of the faded white scar on the side of her throat held him back. Who dared do that to her? Ares would find out and kill him, slowly and painfully, possibly over several weeks. He practically saw his fierce little Omega stabbing at the rogue Lycan with a small potato peeler. Damn, he loved her feistiness.

She'd said she'd rejected the other male, and Ares believed her. She didn't smell like another male. Even if it had been years, his odor would have lingered on her to some degree if she hadn't rejected him.

When they left Andrea's office, Ares insisted on always keeping a hand on her. At first, she seemed annoyed, but gradually, he'd found her relaxing into him over the next hour. She'd touched him twice, though he was sure she didn't realize she did it. It didn't matter. It was only a matter of time before those things became deliberate between them. And if he kept calm and patient, those little touches would become instinct to her.

Twice, he had to hold back a growl when another male kissed her hand and smiled at her. But both times, she shot him a fiery glare, which could make the strongest wolves whimper like a pup and beg forgiveness. He had no idea how she did it. He'd never been cowed by anyone before. Not his parents, and especially not a female. But she wasn't any female. She was his Omega. His other half. His missing piece.

After an hour, a wolf entered looking for her, and River talked to him quietly. He'd glanced at Ares for several seconds before whispering something to her and kissing her hair. He hugged her and exited as Ares lumbered forward and took her arm.

"Who's that?" he demanded.

She pried his grasp from her arm before smiling at the other patrons.

"Firstly, I am not a naughty toddler. Do not grab me. Secondly, that is Bianca's father. My mom's mate."

The man jumped into an old car and drove off.

He flexed his fingers and prayed her arm wouldn't bruise. "I… apologize for grabbing you." He inclined his head to her, and she nodded. "What did he want?"

"None of your business."

Ares growled and went to touch her again, but she slid out of his reach with practiced ease. *Interesting.*

River procured two flutes of champagne from a waiter and

shoved them at him with a bright smile which didn't meet her eyes. "Keep your hands busy somewhere other than my body, please."

"What did he want?" he asked again, trying to calm his voice.

She turned and strode into the gallery without another word.

Ares gripped the crystal flutes so hard one of them cracked. He gulped down both glasses of champagne and slammed them onto a table. He growled as someone joined him.

"Boss."

He turned to Zeke.

"Why don't you go outside for air? I'll make sure she doesn't go anywhere."

"Because you did such a great job before?" he spat.

Zeke stiffened, but his face remained impassive.

Ares was being an ass. But every instinct told him to grab River, throw her over his shoulder, jump into his car, and fly straight to his estate, where he'd keep her locked away from everyone else.

"Some air would be a smart idea." Ares looked at River once more. She mingled and laughed with Bianca and other people in a natural way he'd never possessed.

His wolf grumbled, wanting to go to her. *Mine. Mate. Omega.*

Ares rubbed the ache in his chest and walked out to the street. He sank against the building, sucking in a breath.

His body relaxed a fraction for the first time since entering the art gallery, but his wolf howled as he could no longer smell her.

His phone rang, and he pulled it out.

Vanessa.

He needed a new assistant before River heard rumors about them.

He rejected the call.

The sky had gone dark, and people began to stream out of the gallery when Ares re-entered.

River stood in the back of the gallery amid a heated discussion with Zeke. Zeke touched her arm, and Ares growled, sending several humans scurrying away. Zeke turned, spotted him, and removed his hand.

River eyed Ares and then walked out of view.

Zeke approached him.

"What's happening?" he asked.

"She's… being River."

"Meaning?"

"Meaning she doesn't want to come back to Montreal."

"Not an option."

Zeke nodded. "I understand, but…"

"But what?"

Zeke glanced over his shoulder.

"Spit it out, Zeke."

"You planned on being in town for another week for business anyway. What if we all stayed together in the hotel?"

"No."

Zeke laid his hand on Ares' shoulder. "Here me out. We stay for a week. Let her come to terms with the idea of leaving. Give her time to gather her things and say her goodbyes. The business you have with the packs here is important. And we need their support. Knowing you've taken one of their own as your mate will go a long way with them. But them knowing you are being gentle and considerate of her feelings will go a long way. They need to see you are who you are projecting to be. You are willing to compromise. Word will spread to them if you do this for her."

Ares sucked in a harsh breath and looked to where River and Bianca spoke to a remaining guest.

"Fine. But she stays with me. And she has two guards at all times."

Zeke nodded. "Of course."

The door to the gallery flew open, and a tall woman with wild dark hair burst into the area and scanned it.

"Oh shit," said Zeke.

Zeke ran to the woman. "Cherry-"

"Is that him?" She stormed toward Ares, and Zeke put up his hands to block her. "Are you him? Are you the son of a bitch monster who thinks he can take whatever he wants?"

"Cherry, stop. Please." Zeke tried to gain control of the woman, but her strength and skill surprised Ares.

She shimmied from Zeke's hold and flipped open a butterfly knife from her back pocket.

"I'm gonna carve you up and serve you to my Alpha for dinner, asshole."

She lunged at Ares, but he stepped out of the way. He clutched her by her throat and lifted her off the ground, pinning her to the wall. She swung at him with the knife, and he swatted it out of her hand.

"You dare to try and attack me?"

A soft hand yanked on his arm. His wolf howled, making him pause.

"Stop!" River cried. "Stop. Don't hurt her."

Ares growled at Cherry, but her eyes remained defiant.

"Please," River begged. "Ares, please. I'll go with you. I'll do whatever you want, just don't hurt her."

The terror in her eyes and pleading in her voice made the anger drain out of Ares as if someone had pulled the plug on the bathtub of his soul.

"Highness, please, put her down," Zeke asked.

Ares dropped the woman to her feet, and Cherry enveloped River in her arms. Tears dripped from River's eyes, and pain shot through Ares.

"You can't have her," Cherry said. "You don't deserve her. She's too special for an animal like you."

"Mom." River dried her tears. "It's okay."

Mom? The wildcat woman was River's mother?

"It's not okay," said Cherry. "Strider told me what'd happened, but we have a plan, baby girl. I'm getting you out of here and far away from him."

River hugged her mom a moment more, backed out of her grip, and locked eyes with Ares. "I… I can't."

She dropped her gaze to the floor, and Ares gently entwined his fingers with hers. The caress of her small hands in his made his heartbeat quicken.

"He hasn't marked you yet. You can still go, River. It's like the last one. You rejected him, and we tossed him out. He hasn't been back. You'll see, with distance and time-"

River shook her head. His wolf howled in happiness.

"It's too late," she confessed. "He may not have marked me, but my wolf has made it clear." She shook her head. "There's no running this time. Not from this one."

A soft purr emanated from Ares that he'd never made before meeting River. Somehow, it did something to her. A look of utter bliss had crossed her face the first time he'd done it. And now, as he did it again, she gazed up at him, her eyes soft and inviting.

Cherry's shoulders slumped. "If you so much as harm one hair on my daughter-"

"River is my Beloved. My Omega. Soon to be the High Luna. I would never harm her."

River peeked up at him, her eyes glittering with interest.

Cherry looked as if she had more to say. Instead, she regarded the gallery where River's sculptures stood, and the remaining humans gawked.

"Are those yours?" Cherry asked after a minute.

River nodded.

"Show me."

River met her mother's eyes, and Ares saw her smile for the first time since he'd met her. The sight struck him right in the heart, and he was done. The moment her smile aimed his direction, he would be no more than putty in her hands.

CHERRY AND BIANCA WALKED THROUGH THE GALLERY, WITH RIVER pointing out every piece and explaining how she had altered it. Her mom smiled softly and marveled at River's talent.

"I don't understand," he said to Zeke. "Hasn't she seen River's work before?"

"Bianca said River and her mom have never been close. River's dad was the artistic one. Cherry… tries, but she's not too maternal."

Ares snorted. "Could have fooled me."

"Bianca said Cherry isn't the affectionate type. She said she'd only seen Cherry hug or kiss anyone once before, including Bianca's dad, Strider. And they've been together for over fifteen years. She's an enforcer for their pack."

Ares snorted. If she weren't the mother of his mate, he would have considered making her a hybrid.

Ares folded his arms and watched the women. Cherry's strength resided inside River. She'd taught River to be tough. To protect herself. And he was damn glad she had. Otherwise, River may have ended up with that rogue.

"So, Cherry and Strider aren't mated?"

Zeke shook his head. "They'd both been mated to their fated mates before and lost them. Cherry said she won't go through it again."

Ares had a hard time believing anyone could break Cherry. But a fated mate connection went soul-deep. Hell, though he and River hadn't fully bonded yet, he would never recover if anything happened to her.

After thirty minutes, Andrea approached Ares.

"Uh, Your Highness? I'm getting ready to lock up for the week-end. Did you want to sign the contract for the pieces now or…"

"I'll sign now."

Relief spread across Andrea's face. "Of course. And you and River, did you agree on a price or…"

"I'll pay full price for all of them. Plus, whatever it costs to ship them to my home."

Zeke reached into his pocket, pulled out a matte black business card, and handed it to Andrea.

Andrea smiled. "Of course. Thank you. Give me a moment, and I'll have all the paperwork ready."

Ares nodded but kept his eyes on River. Her hair had tussled out of the clip holding it, and she'd removed her heels. She'd even removed the red lipstick. He took her in, so beautiful and happy. He remembered his mother looking the same after a formal gathering at the estate. Worn out but proud of how all her hard work had paid off.

He swallowed hard. It's been a long time since he'd thought of his mother and all she had gone through after his father's death. The memories made his skin prickle with anger.

"Did you know River had been claimed against her will previously?" he asked.

Zeke growled. "No. I didn't."

"A rogue Lycan."

"What? Who?"

Ares clenched and unclenched his fists. "No idea. But I intend on finding out."

"You give the word, and I'm on it."

River laughed, and Ares' chest squeezed. She brushed her hair over her shoulder, and he practically saw the scar on her throat from across the room. The thought of another male biting her made him want to explode, and he had to take a cleansing breath to clear his head. He would remove the scar with his own mark and spend the rest of their lives making up for it.

"We should go," said Zeke.

Ares nodded, not taking his eyes off River. "Give them another minute."

The way her hair cascaded down her back to the dip in her spine. The way her thin fingers traced the lines of one of the wolves she'd created. Every inch of her perfect. And every inch of her was his- if she'd let him have her.

ARES, ZEKE, AND RIVER RODE TO THE PLAZA HOTEL IN SILENCE. She sat next to him in the limo, gazing out the window so that not even the fabric of her dress touched him. When he shifted his position to be nearer to her, she moved away and laid her head on the window.

Ares sighed.

When they reached the hotel, Zeke got out first, inspected the street, and then stepped to the side for Ares to get out. He instinctively sniffed for trouble before offering his hand to River. She took it, and he helped her out of the car. Unwilling to let her escape from him, he laced his fingers with hers and led her into the lobby of his hotel. As they entered, she gasped, taking the whole thing in.

"Beautiful, isn't it?" he asked as her eyes darted around the structure.

"Exquisite," she whispered.

"I'm glad you like it. It'll be yours as soon as we're mated."

She looked at him but didn't say anything.

He smiled and placed his hand on her lower back as he escorted her through the lobby to the private elevator reserved for guests almost of his status. He was, after all, the owner.

The doors opened, and Vanessa went to step out, but spotted Ares and stopped. She glanced at where Ares and River joined hands.

Zeke stuck his arm out so the elevator door didn't close again.

In the mirrored elevator walls, Ares caught River's expression of distaste at seeing Vanessa.

Vanessa retreated, and Ares led River into the elevator. Zeke stuck a keycard in the penthouse slot.

They rode up in silence for a moment before Ares spoke.

"River, this is my assistant, Vanessa. I don't think you two have been properly introduced. Vanessa, this is my beloved. Her Highness Princess River. You will be at her disposal until we're home."

Vanessa opened her mouth but shut it again.

River refused to make eye contact with her.

"As you wish, Your Highness," Vanessa finally said.

The tension that rose with the elevator told Ares he'd been right. He needed to let Vanessa go as soon as they returned home.

The doors opened to the royal suite. Zeke exited first, and Ares followed with River. The sound of voices met his ears as they entered the foyer. Zeke opened the door, and it opened up to the dining room in front. A corridor to the left ran the length of the suite back to the master bedroom.

"Are you serious?" River asked, looking around.

His men at the dining table stood and bowed to her and Ares.

"River, I would like to introduce you to my bodyguards and most loyal friends."

The men lined up, and Ares introduced them. "This is Theo. He is my oldest friend."

Theo knelt and bowed to River. "Your Highness."

"This is Isaac. He is the youngest of the group but also the most vigilant. He, Lachlan, and Theo will be assigned as your guards whenever you leave my sight."

River bit the inside of her cheek, turned back to the men, and nodded.

"This is Drew. He and Lachlan are the ones who talked to your old Alpha to try and find you in Andover."

"You know Zeke already, and lastly, there is Santiago."

River nodded, and a tense silence settled in between the group.

"Boss, the chef is still here if you and your mate would like something to eat," said Theo.

"Are you hungry?" he asked.

River nodded.

"Have him prepare something and bring it to the master suite."

"Would you like Vanessa to get you anything? She can go anywhere in the city if you need her to."

Vanessa stiffened. She wasn't used to being the one who ran his errands, but more than ever, she had to learn her new place in the house of Wolvenguard.

"I don't need anything," River replied, looking only at him.

His wolf chuffed at River, already asserting her dominance in his pack and household. Good girl.

Ares nodded to Vanessa. "You may go back to your room downstairs. But keep your phone on in case my mate needs anything."

Vanessa's cheeks flamed, but she bowed and left without a word.

Ares led River to the master bedroom and let go of her as he turned to lock the door. She walked to the expansive window and peered out at the night sky.

Something calmed inside him, knowing he had her in his room, in his suite, in his hotel, and under his protection.

Ares stood by the door for a long moment, trying to keep his wolf in check. River stared out over the city, her small, slender form taking up all the oxygen in the room.

His mate. He'd found his mate. An Omega. Having her at his side would make him stable enough to turn the tide of the war with his half-brother.

"You've slept with Vanessa," River said flatly.

Damn. He had been an idiot to think she wouldn't pick up on it.

"I don't want her in my house." River didn't turn from the window.

Her house? They hadn't even gone home yet, and it was already her house.

His wolf chuffed.

"I'll fire her now." He pulled out his phone.

It didn't even ring one full time.

"Ares?" Vanessa said.

River turned.

"You need to pack your things-"

"No," said River. "You have meetings. I am sure you need her for them. You can dismiss her after. But I don't want to see or smell her for the duration of my stay."

Ares nodded. It was beyond generous to allow him to keep Vanessa for his meetings. River truly would make a fantastic Omega.

"Ares?" Vanessa's voice cracked on the line.

"My name is Prince Ares, or Your Highness. You will accompany me to my meetings only while we have another guard. You will be given your own car and driver until we go home. You are not to come up to my suite under any circumstances. You may text me if you need me to talk about business. If it's an emergency, contact Santiago. You will return to Montreal the day before we do. You will clear your things out of the estate and be given thirty days severance as my assistant before you are assigned somewhere else. Do you understand?"

The line remained silent for a long moment as River watched him.

"Yes, Your Highness."

Ares hung up. "Done."

River turned back to the window. "Thank you."

Her words stopped him, and he smiled.

Mine. My Mate. Take her. Claim her.

Ares rubbed his chest. *Don't worry, friend. We will mate her. Just not tonight.*

CHAPTER SEVEN

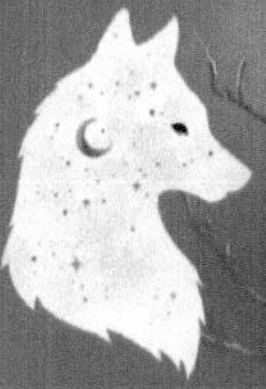

RIVER

River watched the lights twinkle all over the city-brake lights, headlights, stop lights, go lights-people free to go where they wanted and do what they wanted. And as the height of the hotel room separated her from them, so too did her new life.

"Would you like to change?" Ares asked.

The sound of his voice sent a shiver of desire through her, but she shut it down like an unwanted slap to the ass.

"You have something I can wear?" She didn't turn.

"Uh… well… there's a bathrobe in the salon if you would like to bathe. There's a beautiful antique claw tub with all kinds of… things, soaps, and whatnot."

She pressed her forehead to the cool glass. Every particle of her sagged with exhaustion. A hot bath did sound wonderful.

"All right." She turned from the window when Ares' sudden

movement caught her off guard. He knelt before her and wrapped her in his bulky arms.

Her heartbeat hammered as she stood, hands in the air, unsure of what to do. Part of her wanted to push him away; the other part wanted to know if his muscles were as cut as she thought they would be.

After a minute, he stood and turned from her. She stared at his hunched shoulders for a moment, unsure of what to say, so she walked to the bathroom and shut the door behind herself, locking it.

She turned the water on in the tub with shaking fingers, took off her dress, curled in a ball on the white marble floor, and sobbed.

THIRTY MINUTES LATER, A KNOCK ON THE DOOR PULLED HER OUT OF her bath.

"River, the food is ready," said Ares.

She wondered if he would try to open the door, but the handle didn't move.

"Thank you," she called.

She listened for his footsteps to recede before letting the water out of the tub and stepping onto a plush bathmat. She plucked a towel from the rack and tossed her hair up before tying a robe around herself.

She pulled the robe shut as much as possible and double-knotted the tie, not that it would stop him if he decided he wanted to take her.

When she left the bathroom, she found a table with beautiful china and a candelabra.

Her stomach roared. The outer door opened, and Ares returned with a bottle of champagne and two glasses.

She sucked in a sharp breath at the sight of him. He'd removed his suit coat and dress shirt, revealing a white tank stretched as far as his muscles would let it go. He'd removed his belt, socks, and shoes and stood barefoot in the doorway as he ducked and turned sideways to enter. Even Zeke wasn't so tall as to have to do that.

"Feeling better?"

No. "Yes, thank you, Highness."

He shook his head and put the bottle and glasses on the table. "My name is Ares. Just Ares. Not Prince Ares. Not Highness or Majesty or anything else. I am Ares. Your Ares."

She couldn't wrap her head around the fact that he considered himself 'Her Ares'. She didn't consider herself 'His River'.

"Sit." He pulled out the chair for her, and she crossed to the table and sat. He lifted her chair off the ground a few inches and moved her closer to the table.

Damn, he's strong. For a moment, she imagined what his skillful hands might do to her.

Her wolf chuffed at the thought of his wolf's strength. *Protector. Provider. Mate.*

No. Stop it! Don't think about him like that. He's a monster, and you are now his property. Nothing more.

He lifted the silver cover off her plate, and her mouth watered. A colossal steak, small potatoes, veggies, and more sat in front of her.

She dug in before Ares returned to his seat.

"I'm glad you're hungry," he said. "Because this is the first course."

The first course?

They ate silently for several minutes with Ares watching her devour everything on her plate. If this had been a first date with a regular shifter, she wouldn't have dared eat so much and so quickly, but hell, he was supposed to be her mate, right? Better he saw what he'd gotten himself into.

He poured champagne into her glass, and she gulped it down. He filled it again, a slight smile playing on his lips.

"I'll be sure to tell the chef you enjoy his cooking," he chuckled.

She shrugged and snatched a fresh roll.

"So, tell me about yourself."

She gulped her champagne and the roll down hard.

"Why? In time, you'll find it all out anyway. No need to give it all up tonight."

His smile turned to a scowl. "Okay. Tell me one thing about yourself."

She tried to gauge whether he was genuinely interested or making conversation. His eyes gave nothing away, so she thought for a moment. "I don't like to be forced to do things I don't want to."

He growled. "Let me clarify. Tell me one thing about yourself I don't already know."

"How am I supposed to do that? Seems you found out about my show quite easily. You might have bought a file from the FBI and learned everything down to the color of the underwear I'm wearing."

"You aren't wearing underwear." He smirked.

River pulled her robe closer around her and crossed her legs. "See, you already know everything."

Ares slammed his fist on the table, shaking the glassware. She didn't jump; she was used to Cherry's outbursts. Instead, she moved the food around her plate and waited for him to say something.

Childish pup. Stubborn. Her wolf huffed.

River knew she acted like a petulant child but was too exhausted to care. He'd shown up, demanding she come with him back to Canada without asking what she wanted or getting her feelings on the subject. It was damn obvious he already wanted to bite her and make her his mate, but he hadn't once asked her opinion about the whole thing.

He took a long, slow breath and gave her a stiff smile.

"Tell me what made you choose metal as your medium for artistic expression."

His statement caught her off guard, and she popped a small potato into her mouth.

"My dad taught me how to work with my hands. He was a mechanic, and he had scraps of metal lying around. One day, I picked up a torch and started messing with a steel tube. I liked the way I bent it to my will and made it more beautiful than a plain piece of scrap metal that would have otherwise been thrown in the trash."

He watched her intently. Was he interested in her more than just to have sex with her to strengthen himself and his position as well as make her pop out babies?

"I heard your dad died. I'm so sorry. How did that happen?"

River's chest squeezed like a Victorian corset. "Uh... my dad was an Alpha but never wanted to lead. Even so, the Alpha of our pack felt threatened by him because our other pack members would turn to him for guidance and help. So, he set my dad up as a traitor and executed him in an unfair fight."

Ares stared at her. "I'm... so sorry."

She nodded. "Me too."

"I don't remember hearing anything like that. What happened to your Alpha?"

River licked her lips. "My mother took care of him."

River would never forget the night her mom came home covered in the Alpha's blood. She'd not said a word; just went into her room and closed the door. The next day, Strider and Bianca had come to live with them.

"What about you," she asked. "What do you do? Besides slaughtering shifters who step out of line?"

He lifted his champagne to his lips but stopped. "Is that what you think?"

"Am I wrong?"

He gulped down the champagne before folding his ample arms across. "No. But that's not all I do."

"Okay."

"Yes. My family is the law. We are the ruling class for the Lycan and shifter society. That isn't always a pleasant or fun job, River, but if we don't enforce the laws, imagine the chaos that would reign worldwide. It's only been in the last hundred years that we've convinced humans we don't exist. With all the unrest among the humans alone, what do you think would happen if the majority discovered shifters, Lycans, vampires, and more were real?"

Sadly, she couldn't argue with him.

"But to answer your question. I went to school for banking and securities. It has allowed my family to provide for ourselves and now for you."

"I don't want your money."

"Maybe, but you aren't complaining about the food. Or the bath. Or the imported bathrobe." Irritation seethed through his words.

"Would you like me to regurgitate the meal? I'd take the robe off, but I'm afraid of what you might take that as a sign of."

He raked his hands into his hair. "Are you always like this?"

"Like what?"

"So.... Infuriating."

She tossed him her most winning smile and batted her eyelashes. "Yup."

He got up from the table and stormed to the door. He paused as he reached it and turned back.

"For the record, Little Wolf, you aren't the only one who didn't ask for this match. If I'd had my way, I would have been mated years ago to a submissive, soft mate who liked nothing more than keeping my bed warm and tending to our pups."

"Well," said River. "Too bad you're stuck with a bitch whose bite is worse than her bark. And I always have cold feet, so you might want to wear pants in bed."

He twisted the locked doorknob so hard it broke off, and the door swung inward. He slammed it behind himself, but it bounced open again.

River held back a laugh as he stormed out of sight.

She dropped her gaze to her plate, and her stomach roiled. Her wolf grumbled at her and curled into a ball.

"Don't talk to me," she said. "I didn't ask you for your opinion anyway."

Her wolf's fur bristled, and she turned away from River.

River sighed and lifted the bottle of champagne before heading to the bed and plopping down on it.

Perhaps he didn't want the mating bond as much as she had thought. The idea made her wolf whine.

River took a long swig of the champagne, knowing it wouldn't do anything to her. She pushed down the duvet and curled in a ball under the sheets.

A mate. She had a mate. A sinfully sexy, powerfully terrifying mate. And she wanted absolutely nothing to do with him.

CHAPTER EIGHT

RIVER

The following day, River opened her eyes to find racks and racks of clothing, shoes, and coats lined up in the room.

She blinked twice before getting up from the bed and wondering how the hell she'd slept through all of it arriving. She pulled the bedsheet with her and walked to the first rack.

She thumbed through the designer dresses, rompers, and suits, looking at each price tag.

"Price is no object if you like something," said a voice from the corner.

River spun around to find Ares' taut form lying on the floor on a makeshift bed.

"I can't wear these," she said. "Each one costs more than my rent."

His eyes remained closed. "As I said, cost isn't a problem. Take what you like unless you intend on wearing the sheet all day."

She swallowed, realizing she wasn't wearing anything underneath the sheet.

"There's bags of underwear and bras on the table."

River glanced at the table where at least a dozen Victoria's Secret bags sat.

She'd always loved Victoria's Secret and Pink, but she'd only been able to afford a few things when on double clearance. Interest piqued, she tiptoed to the table and peeked in the first bag. She couldn't help the smile that spread across her face as she pulled out a matching black lace bra and panty set.

"Did I do well?"

Ares' warm breath tickled her shoulder, and she whirled around to face him. It'd been a bad idea. Ares stood in front of her, wearing nothing but skintight boxer briefs that barely covered the tops of his thighs.

She couldn't take her eyes off his body as every chiseled muscle of his torso blocked everything else out of view.

Her cheeks heated as she took in every ripped and cut muscle of his body from his neck to his toes. Her fingers twitched, wanting to touch his skin, and her wolf sprung to life, wanting his body pressed against hers. Inside her. His fangs buried in her neck, and his knot filling her.

When her gaze met his, she couldn't stop the overwhelming desire that flushed her skin and made her innermost lady parts thrum.

Ares pushed her hair over her shoulder. The lightness of his fingers made her quiver, and her body heat further. He traced his fingers down her arm and up her stomach. He brushed over her nipple through the sheet, making her heartbeat thunder. Without thinking, she gripped him by the neck and pulled his mouth to hers.

She clung to him as he cupped her rear and lifted her onto the table. She wrapped her legs around his waist, and he kissed her harder. She gripped his shoulders, and her nails lengthened as she dug into his back.

A sound between a growl and a sigh escaped him. Brushing the bags onto the floor, he laid her back and stepped between her thighs before caging her body with his.

His length rubbed against her core, making her pant with need. Every nerve of her body screamed out for her to bite him. To mark him. To make him hers. And to allow him to mark her in return. He circled his hips into hers, making her mewl.

He pinned her wrists above her head with one hand as he ripped off his underwear and ground against her through the thin, silky fabric she'd slept on.

He slid his tongue down the side of her throat and suckled one of her breasts through the sheet.

Stop, her mind screamed. *Stop being so weak. You don't even know him.*

But her wolf squelched the thoughts spurring her onward.

"Ares," she panted.

Ares worked his way back up to her throat and flicked his warm tongue over the tendon at her collarbone.

"Tell me," he demanded.

"Ares."

"Tell me," he said again. "Tell me you want me to mark you. That you want to be mine forever."

He licked her throat, and his fangs grazed her skin, bringing her back to reality. She stiffened at the sensation of his sharp canines on her skin.

No! No way! She wasn't ready.

"River-"

"No," she said sharply.

He nuzzled her neck, sending panic tumbling through her. Memories flashed, and dark eyes stared at her from the other side of the pantry door.

"I said no!" she shouted.

The sudden sound of footsteps rushing to the room pulled Ares' mouth from her skin. The door flung open, and Zeke, Lachlan, and Theo rushed in.

Ares roared, and Zeke aimed his weapon at Ares.

"Back away from her," Zeke commanded.

"Get out! She's mine."

"No," said Theo. "She's your intended; there is a difference. We all heard her. She said no. It is forbidden to take a mate without her consent."

"Those are Lycan laws; she's a shifter."

Zeke steadied his aim on Ares. "Don't make me do it, Boss. Please don't. I know what you are feeling right now, but she said no. If you cross this line, you will lose her forever."

River's heart hammered as Ares' grip tightened on her body.

"Please, Your Highness," said Lachlan. "This isn't you. You know it isn't."

"I take what I want."

"Not this time, Ares. Not like this," said Theo.

Ares stared down at her, his all-black eyes as terrifying as the inhumane expression on his face.

He took her in. His eyes cleared, and he let go of her.

She scrambled backward on the table, pressing her palm to her skin to see if he'd drawn blood.

His expression shifted, and he stalked out of the room before she said a word.

River's breathing came in and out in harsh bursts.

When a door slammed across the suite, she almost fell off the table. Zeke steadied her, and she clung to him.

"Zeke," Theo warned.

"He's my sister's mate. He's basically my brother," she yelled. "Leave."

Theo glanced between Zeke and River and then nodded to Lachlan. The two exited the room, leaving the door open.

Zeke wrapped his arm around River's shoulders. "Are you hurt?"

She shook her head, weaker and more out of control than ever.

He released her and pushed her to arm's length. "Your mother would have my balls for dinner if I let anything happen to you. I'm sure Bianca would, too."

River let out a harsh laugh and nodded. Memories bombarded her again.

The bite. The pain. Stabbing and stabbing and stabbing with the potato peeler. Her wolf screaming at her.

"Not him! Not this one!"

"Why don't you find something to wear? We need to have a conversation."

River blinked back tears which threatened to spill, and she touched her neck again. He hadn't done it. He'd stopped. But not of his own accord. If Theo and Zeke hadn't been there… Would he have stopped?

Zeke picked the bags off the floor and pulled out a velour track-suit with the word Pink on the butt. He handed it to her, and she bit her tongue at the protest forming in her mouth.

"Thank you." She took the outfit, grabbed some underwear off the floor, and shuffled to the bathroom to dress.

ARES

"I EXPLAINED OUR LAWS TO HER," ZEKE SAID. "I TOLD HER SHE MUST say yes to you marking her. She understands if she doesn't, and you mark her or try to take her, it is a death sentence."

Ares hung his head in his hands. He didn't want to feel this way. He didn't want to want River. Had she not been his mate, he would have noticed her extreme beauty and tried to take her into his bed, but he'd never imagined letting her into his head and to his wolf the way she did.

But he couldn't help it. She was an Omega- his Omega. Everything about her sang to him like his own private melody. But how? She should have been submissive- she wasn't. She should have fallen at his feet- she didn't. She should have been overjoyed to have been chosen to be his- not even slightly. How? How could he want her so badly it made his muscles ache, and yet she couldn't stand to be in the same room as him?

"Did I hurt her?" Ares asked.

"No."

Ares nodded. Well, there was that at least. When his wolf took over, there was no telling what he'd do. And if he hurt her… the council's punishment wouldn't begin to hurt as much as the knowledge that he'd done something to her. Her terrified eyes when she'd seen him barely wolfed out had been like a cold, wet rag to the nether regions. It had almost broken him to see her so scared and know he'd made her afraid.

"I think it's better if I move into another suite for the remainder of our stay," said Ares.

"Boss-"

Ares stood and straightened his tie. "I have meetings today, and I need to make sure things are running smoothly at home. Please make sure River has everything she needs. I'll take the suite next door."

"Don't you want me to come with you?"

Ares whipped his suit jacket from the back of his chair. "I'll take Santiago and Drew."

"Boss-"

"Take her wherever she wants to go. Just make sure she is back before dark." Ares dug into his pocket and pulled out his wallet. "And take this. Buy her whatever she requires." He handed Zeke his credit card and made for the door.

"Ares."

Ares stopped without turning.

"She will come around. You need to be patient."

"Why is it me who has to be patient?" he asked. "Why can't she get with the program?"

"Because that's not how it works, unfortunately. You have to understand, shifters have been taught to fear Lycans from birth. Lycans are the boogeymen under the bed. It takes time to break down years of indoctrination. Yes, her body wants you. Yes, her wolf wants you. But in her head, you are still the executioner of shifters."

"But I'm not the one who started those rumors, and I'm not the one who keeps trying to perpetuate them. That's why I'm here to meet with the Alphas. I'm trying to break those rumors."

"I understand. And I know that now, but it took me time too, when I met you. Same with the others. She doesn't know yet. But she will. Just like we know."

"So, what do I do, Zeke?"

"Firstly? Try to control your temper. River may like a take-charge guy, but she doesn't like being scared of him."

"I would never hurt her." Even as the words left his mouth, he realized he'd been ready to an hour before.

"Show her."

Ares turned to the door again. "Make sure they have my suite ready for tonight. I don't know when I'll be back."

He walked out of the second bedroom and down the hall to the sitting room. He smelled River in the master bedroom but didn't dare say goodbye.

"Drew, Santiago, let's go."

He stalked to the suite entrance. *Damn. It would be a long day.*

RIVER

River spent the day in her room. Within fifteen minutes of the suite door slamming shut, it flew open again with a bang, and her bedroom door flung inward. She stiffened, waiting for a verbal barrage. But it wasn't Ares, it was Bianca. Tear-streaked face, makeup, and hair untamed, she burst into the room and ran to River.

"I'm so sorry, sis. I'm so sorry. I didn't know. It's all my fault. I should never have made you come out with us. I didn't know." Bianca flung her arms around River.

River hugged her little sister and squeezed her eyes shut. She wanted to break down. She wanted to bawl her eyes out, too, but she couldn't. She had to be in control for both of them.

"It's okay, B. It's not your fault. None of this is your fault. It would have happened sooner or later. I had hoped it would be later, much later."

Bianca searched River's face, wiping the tears from her cheeks. Her face scrunched up, and she pinched River hard.

"Ow!"

"Why didn't you tell me?"

"Cherry and Strider didn't want me to. They didn't want anyone to know."

"You could have told me. I wouldn't have let it slip."

River pushed the dark hair from her little sister's eyes. "I know, B."

Bianca chewed her lip. "Are you... did he..."

River shook her head, remembering Ares' eyes. "No. I thought he might, but he didn't."

Bianca flung her arms around River again. This time, as Bianca hugged her, River hugged her fiercely. Her emotions swirled inside her as her wolf glowered at her. How the hell did she live when half of her wanted to be free, and the other half wanted to be his?

After several minutes, Bianca let go and went to the racks. She chewed her bottom lip, and River chuckled.

"Go on. You're dying to go through them."

Bianca's eyes shone. "Are you sure? He won't be mad?"

River's brows knit. "I don't care if he does. They are mine. He said so. If I want to light them on fire or donate them to charity, that's my choice."

Horror crossed Bianca's features. "You wouldn't dare. They're designer."

"Take anything you want."

RIVER AND BIANCA SPENT THE MORNING CHATTING AND TRYING things on. Surprisingly, River liked more than half the things Ares had picked for her. Eating a burger and fries, she wondered how and where Ares had gotten all those things late at night. Did he have Victoria's Secret on speed dial or something? The thought made her wolf growl. River didn't want to think of Ares having a lingerie store on speed dial so he could buy his latest conquest whatever he wanted, whenever he wanted. The thought of him with another female made River's wolf rise to her feet for the first time in hours and let out a warning growl so possessive it scared River.

Mine. My mate. My Alpha.

River rubbed her chest at the sudden surge of anger that flooded her. *Yeah, yeah. I get it.*

Her wolf glared at her as if telling her to hurry up already. But River wasn't sure she wanted to hurry up. She had a life in New York. A job. A job she loved. And though Ares had swooped in and bought all of her sculptures, others had wanted to buy her art. Rich people. Important people. And she was leaving all of it behind, why? For a man? Okay, not just a man. A super-hot melt-your-panties-off-with-a-glance man. His eyes floated into her mind, and the way he'd touched her. She craved his touch again like she'd never craved anything. The feel of his giant hands sliding up her thigh, under her dress, and down-

"We should go out," Bianca announced, pulling River from her thoughts.

"Uh… not today, B. I'm exhausted."

Bianca smiled and bounded over to the bed, bouncing on it. "Movie marathon!"

River smiled. "Yes."

Bianca plopped down beside her and lay back on the pillows. "Rom coms. Or holiday romances. Something fun and light."

River nodded. Romances weren't her thing when it came to movies. She wasn't in the mood to see people fall in love, but she didn't want to ruin Bianca's day. Bianca remained on cloud ten with her impending mating to Zeke, and River didn't want to ruin it for her because of her own messed-up situation.

"Holidays," she said, and Bianca smiled and reached for the remote.

Bianca clicked on the enormous flat screen and called for Zeke. As if standing right outside the door waiting for her to beckon, the door opened, and he walked in, giving River a slight bow before turning his sparkling eyes on Bianca. The adoration shining through his eyes made River's heart clench. Ares had looked at her the same way the night they'd met in the club.

She didn't want to think about Ares. But how the heck did she not, when his delicious scent lingered in the room, and she wore the clothing he'd bought her and ate the food he provided?

"Zeke, we need movie stuff."

His eyebrows scrunched. "Movie stuff?"

"You know," said Bianca. "Popcorn, candy, soda. Movie stuff."

He smiled. "Of course, my love."

Bianca blushed and chewed her bottom lip. The air between them heated.

Her wolf grumbled. *Ares. Mine.*

River rolled her eyes.

By the time they'd seen four movies, River needed a break. The clock read seven p.m. Ares should be back soon. Shouldn't he? She stood from the lush bed and cleaned up the wrappers from all the candy they'd eaten and half a dozen soda cans. She didn't want him to think she was a total slob.

She stopped, realizing she cared what he thought of her. She'd never cared what people thought of her before.

"What do you want to do now?" River asked.

"You mean you're done?" Bianca's mouth pulled into a frown.

River couldn't remember the last time she'd relaxed and binged movies. A year? More? All she'd done was work since moving to New York and starting school. The knowledge she had no commitments to anything both scared and intrigued her. Her high school summers were the last time she'd had no commitments.

River smiled. "I wondered if you wanted to do something else."

"Like what?"

River shrugged. "I need to leave this room. I need air."

Bianca stood. "There's a patio with a hot tub and pool. We should swim."

River wasn't up for swimming, but a soak would be glorious. She nodded.

"I'll have to borrow a swimsuit," said Bianca.

"No need to borrow. Take one. I can't imagine a world where I'd need all five."

Bianca ran to the rack without being told twice, yanked a gold bikini off the hook, and looked at River expectantly.

"Go for it."

The thing would barely cover Bianca's curvy assets, and River couldn't wait to see Zeke's reaction.

Bianca squealed and tossed off her maxi dress.

River, too, went to the rack and thumbed through the suits. She settled on the least revealing one: a black halter one-piece with cut-out sides.

Several minutes later, she and Bianca emerged from the bedroom with towels slung over their shoulders and headed to the front room. The aromas of the men who had stayed all day permeated the spacious suite. She caught Ares' sultry scent, and that somehow disappointed her.

They emerged into the front room, and the men glanced over from a football game they'd been watching. Theo choked on his beer and spat it out on the floor before averting his eyes. Lachlan's cheeks flushed, and he, too, turned away, but it was Zeke's reaction River found most amusing. Bianca gave him a huge smile and ran to him, kissing him hard. Zeke kissed her back. Pulling her arms from around his neck, he wrapped the towel around her.

"Bianca! What are you doing?" he demanded.

Bianca's face fell. "River and I are going swimming."

Zeke glanced at River and then away. "You… you can't come out here dressed or not dressed, I should say."

Bianca frowned. "You don't like my suit?"

Zeke growled and looked over his shoulder at Theo and Lachlan, who studied a painting on the wall with particular interest.

"I fricking love the suit but…"

"But what?"

"But you should not be out amongst other males wearing practically nothing," came a booming voice behind them.

River swung around to find Ares standing with Santiago and Drew in the doorway. Both of whom stared pointedly at their shoes.

Ares' heated gaze raked over River's body, and she wrapped her own towel around herself, though every ounce of her wanted him to look at her. To see her. To want her.

What? Where the hell had that come from?

Ares growled as his eyes stayed on River, and the four bodyguards, minus Zeke, walked straight out of the suite.

Ares didn't move. He didn't make another sound. He simply watched River, his eyes hungry. His impeccably tailored suit fit his frame meticulously. His dark waves had been slicked back, and his jaw sported a few days of stubble, which had been groomed to fit the hard angles of his face. She wondered if he did it or had someone else do it. He was the perfect mix of hot male model and bad boy biker.

Suddenly, she didn't want to soak in the hot tub with Bianca. She wanted to soak in the hot tub with Ares. To see those rippling, tanned muscles and feel his hands grab her once again.

Nope! Stop. Don't go there.

River's arousal grew so fast she wasn't sure if she'd been heading for the hot tub or if she'd already been in it.

"Did... your meetings go well?" she asked, trying to slice through the tension.

Ares nodded but still didn't speak.

"You two go out on the patio," said Zeke. "I'll order everyone some food. Then we can have dinner together." He pecked Bianca on the cheek and moved her toward the sliding doors.

"Are you coming, sis?"

River watched Ares. What the hell was she waiting for? She didn't need his permission.

She waited another few seconds to see if Ares would say something. When he didn't, she walked out the sliding glass door and entered the warm hot tub, wishing for an icy shower instead.

CHAPTER NINE

ARES

Ares didn't move from where he'd been standing for at least five minutes. Didn't move. Didn't speak. Simply breathed. His wolf had begun to break his restraints, and his nails had lengthened in his pockets, slashing holes in them. His fangs had extended as well as the sight of River, but he'd forced them to stop. He'd scared her enough for one day.

As he watched through the door, he fought every instinct that told him to take her and make her his. Her perfume swirled around him like a boa, constricting his chest and crushing it inward.

Somehow, her scent had grown exponentially more robust in the hours he'd been away. Probably because she hadn't taken blockers. Blockers no longer mattered anyway since she was his, and he'd make damn sure everyone knew it.

His wolf snarled and clawed to be released, but Ares refused. He wouldn't lose control again. No matter how much his wolf wanted her. No matter how much he wanted her. He wasn't going to let it happen again. He wouldn't be one of those Lycans. He was trying to make peace with the shifters, not alienate them further.

Zeke walked up to Ares and held out a glass. Ares took it without removing his eyes from where River soaked in the hot tub alongside her sister. Her silvery hair fanned out over the patio tile like a bridal veil as she stared up at the stars, pointing and smiling.

Ares downed the liquid in one quick, fiery burst. Zeke looked at his glass and handed it to Ares while taking the first one from Ares' hand.

Ares gulped down the liquid again, letting it burn through his gut, but he barely noticed it next to the fire already smoldering inside.

"What should I order for dinner?" Zeke asked.

Ares shook his head. "I'll eat in my suite. I only stopped by to grab a suit and to…" To what? To see if River had changed? To see if she was ready to bond with him? "To grab a suit," he finished.

Zeke stood next to Ares, watching the two women. Ares' wolf snarled.

The two women splashed each other. River dunked Bianca, and when she jumped back up, River's breasts bobbed up and down, making Ares' pants tighten as his arousal struck him like a wrecking ball.

Zeke chuckled as Bianca surfaced, and Ares' wolf almost lashed out at him for watching the women.

"What are you looking at? Ares asked.

Zeke coughed. "Uh… my mate and my soon-to-be sister-in-law."

A moment passed as the words rattled around Ares' brain, calming his wolf.

"Why?" asked Zeke. "What are you looking at?"

Ares glanced at Zeke. A smile played across his lips.

"I'm looking at my mate. And my soon-to-be sister-in-law." Despite himself, Ares snorted, and so did Zeke.

"So, will we be related?" Zeke asked.

"Depends."

"On what?"

"On whether you want to be pulled deeper into the crapstorm of my family."

Zeke snorted and turned back to the sliding glass door. "Actually, I think I'm okay. Taking on Cherry as a mother-in-law is all I can handle for now."

Ares groaned. Cherry would be his mother-in-law, too. "I don't blame you. To be honest, I'd rather deal with my crap than have to deal with Cherry again."

Zeke snickered. "Do you think she will warm up to us?"

Ares cocked an eyebrow. "Do feral house cats ever warm up to lions?"

Zeke thought for a moment. "Sorry, are we the feral house cats or the lions?"

"No clue."

The women got out of the hot tub and toweled off. That was Ares' cue.

"I'll see you tomorrow. Take care of them for me."

Zeke inclined his head. "With my life."

Ares clapped Zeke on the shoulder. With his wolf howling, Ares went to gather a few things for the night and following day.

And then… he'd go for a jog. A long, muscles burning, heart pounding, keep going till his legs gave out jog. One meant to drop him into bed and forget all about the fact that his Omega, River, lay in a bed a hundred feet from him.

RIVER

When River reentered the suite, Ares no longer stood staring at her and Bianca. She'd gone out to the hot tub to relax, but from the moment Ares had made his presence known, she'd been able to do anything but. Her wolf stood on high alert, clocking his every movement and wanting only to be closer to him.

But River refused to look at him, hoping he'd grow bored and leave. Which he apparently had because when she'd gotten out of the water and dried off, he'd been gone.

Now, sitting at the dinner table with Bianca and Zeke, listening to them chatter about mating ceremony details, River couldn't do anything more than push her food around her plate and continually glance sideways at the empty chair where Ares should be.

After twenty minutes, River couldn't take any more. "When will Ares be back?" she blurted, interrupting Bianca.

Zeke looked at her. "Ares is gone for the night. I'm sorry."

River's body flushed with heat. "For the night? You mean with another female?"

"No. Not at all." Zeke's eyes widened. "I mean, he only stopped by to pack a few things. That's all."

"Pack a few things?" She didn't understand.

"Ares has gotten another suite across the hall. He thought you would prefer to have your own space."

A chill rained down on River. Her own space? They hadn't been together for two days, and already he'd had enough of her. River laid down her fork and took a long sip of her wine. Conflict rooted in her breast. Wasn't that what she wanted? Him to reject her and let her go? Or did she? She couldn't deny the attraction between their wolves, nor her attraction to him in general. He was the most handsome man she'd ever met. But at the same time, she had a life in New York, and she liked being able to do what she wanted.

And yet… She'd always hoped for a fated mate. Always hoped to find someone who looked at her the way Strider did at her mom. Someone who became her whole world. Someone to love and protect her against everything. The kind of connection that could never break. With someone who would never leave her. Someone all her own.

River stood. "I think I'm going to go to bed. I'm tired."

Bianca stood. "Do you want company?"

River shook her head. "You and Zeke need time together. Besides, if you are coming to Canada with me, we'll see more of each other from now on. Enough that you'll get sick of me." River forced a smile, but the words hurt more than she could say.

"Never River. I love that we'll be together again." Bianca stepped toward River, but Zeke gripped her wrist, and Bianca sat back in her chair.

"River. It may not be my place, but I need to tell you. Ares may be overbearing and aggressive, but he is also loyal and kind-hearted. If he weren't, I never would have agreed to be turned by him or to work with him. I understand the bond isn't what you want, but you shouldn't let that get in the way of the happiness you can have with your fated mate."

Now, what the hell did she say?

She nodded to Zeke, turned, and shuffled to the bedroom. The blanket still lay on the floor where Ares had slept the night before. She walked to it without knowing why and lay down on it, pulling his scent into her nostrils. Every muscle relaxed, and within minutes, she fell asleep.

ARES

"I'M TELLING YOU, HIGHNESS, SHE IS CURLED IN A BALL ON THE floor in the makeshift bed you made, asleep."

Ares paced his suite. He didn't want to be away from River working on business all day, and now, back at the hotel, his wolf demanded to check on her.

The marathon had not weakened Ares' wolf or what he wanted. In a weird way, it made his wolf more agitated since all he wanted was for River to run with him. He wanted nothing more than to take her home to his estate and explore the woods surrounding his house with her. Okay, there was one thing he wanted to be doing more. He wanted to wrap himself around her naked in his bed.

Stop!

"Go look," said Zeke. "I'm not lying to you. When you weren't at dinner, she didn't eat."

"Perhaps she wasn't hungry."

"Then why did she keep looking at your vacant seat? And why did she ask about you?"

Ares didn't want to get his hopes up. Couldn't get his hopes up. He needed to lock it all down. Everything inside him screamed for him to go to her. Every instinct his feral wolf had was to take, claim, mate, rut. But he couldn't. It was the hardest thing he'd ever done. It took more willpower than he knew he had not to take her, but if he did, she would never be his. And most likely, Cherry would sneak into his house one night and cut his throat.

"Keeping away from her isn't going to make this any better," Theo offered.

Ares regarded his men. "But it will keep her safe."

"From you?" Theo asked.

Ares nodded. "I can't control my wolf around her. Her scent. Her taste. The urges in me… I understand why that rogue bit her. It's horrible, but I do understand."

"You have to learn to control it," said Theo.

Ares growled.

"I've known you longer than anyone," Theo said. "And I get it. You are the heir to the Lycan throne and the biggest badass of all of us. You are used to getting whatever you want when you want it. But that's gonna change now."

"What do you mean?"

"I mean, you have a mate. Having a mate isn't about what you always want, but what they want. Right now, you want what your wolf wants. It's what all of us want when we find our mate. But you must think with your human head and not your Lycan instinct. River isn't like other Omegas. She isn't going to roll over and play submissive. She wasn't raised that way. You have to be slow with her, gentle. Let her get to know you."

Ares rubbed his hands over his face. He'd never let a woman in before. His men knew him because they'd been through hell together on multiple occasions. But he'd only ever entertained women for one thing, and it wasn't to get to know him.

He hissed out a harsh breath. But for some reason, he wanted her to. To learn everything about him. To bandage up the broken parts and make the decent parts better. He wanted… her.

ARES OPENED HIS SUITE DOOR AND STOPPED. VANESSA STOOD, HAND raised, ready to knock.

"What are you doing here?" Ares had seen little of her the last two days, and it surprised him how much he liked it when she wasn't around.

Vanessa was the best assistant he'd ever had, but a terrible friend with benefits. As has been made apparent in the less than three minutes she and River had spent in the elevator together. He'd not missed her at all over the past two days. Not driving in the car. Not sitting next to him at his meetings. Not listening to her make phone calls for him and schmooze people, nothing. None of it. And in that moment, looking at her standing at his door, he understood why. There wasn't any drama that came along with her just being her.

"I asked what you needed," said Ares.

She pulled a bottle of wine from behind her back. "I overheard the guys saying you got your own suite, so I came to see if you wanted some company." The flippant way she said it grated his nerves.

"I'm on my way to the other suite right now. I only moved over here as a courtesy to my mate because her sister has been staying with her for the last day or so."

A smile twisted the corner of her mouth. “Do you have any idea what new *position* you want me in when we return to Montreal?"

His wolf's hackles raised, and he snarled.

Ares choked back the scathing retort he had for her and instead said, "I might be opening an office in Europe. If I do, I'll need to send someone I trust to head it up. And they will certainly need an assistant, especially one as fluent in as many languages as you are. You put a lot of work into all those courses. Time to put them to use."

Her mouth fell open. "Europe? You... you want to send me to Europe?"

"You always said you wanted to go. This would be the perfect opportunity. Travel. Pay. And it would be hard for your home pack Alpha to reach you there. Unfortunately, with you not being my assistant, I won't be able to guarantee your safety from him."

Her cheeks flushed. "Why? Why are you doing this to me, Ares? Five years. I've been loyal to you for five years and-"

"And you knew when you started this would happen. I didn't lie to you or lead you on, Vanessa. I always told you I was searching for my mate. I searched every chance I got. I told you before you climbed into my bed for the first time, this was friends with benefits, nothing more. You agreed to it. As a matter of fact, we signed a contract to avoid any misunderstanding. Do you need me to print you a copy?"

"I thought you'd change your mind. Stop looking. Choose me."

"What did I ever do to give you that impression? When did I ever talk with you about my hopes, my dreams? What I wanted from the future? Name one time you ever spent the night in my bed or I in yours. When have we ever gone to dinner that wasn't a meeting? When have we ever attended an event that wasn't for business? When have we ever seen a movie together? Or walked in the park? Or go for a run in the woods?"

She swallowed hard. "Never."

"That's right. Not once in five years. So please tell me what I did to make you think we were anything more than what we originally agreed to be?"

Anger blazed behind her green eyes. Fair enough. Let her be angry. If she'd started crying, he'd never have believed it. The anger, though, was all her.

"When will you admit the only reason you ever took this job was for the protection it offered you, the status, and the perks? You don't want me. You want my title. You want my money. You want the power. I've known from the first day you came to work. And those things made you an acceptable assistant. But those same things meant you would never be my mate."

Ares padded softly across the hall and tapped his keycard on the lock of the suite without waiting for Vanessa to say anything more. It beeped and turned green, and he pressed open the door. He stood for a moment and breathed River in. Shutting his eyes, he let the feelings wash over him. His wolf stood, but Ares shoved him down.

No. Not this time. Not again. He would not let his wolf take over.

Ares turned left, walked past where his men sat, and headed for the bedroom. His bare feet clapped against the cold marble floor, but his temperature remained hot as ever, especially knowing he would see her.

He walked up to the door and stopped. He reached for the knob, half believing it would be locked, but when he tried the newly replaced handle, it turned downward. Ares swung the door in lightly and peered into the darkened room. His heartbeat kicked up as he searched the bed for her, but she wasn't there. His gaze drifted to the floor, and sure enough, down where he'd slept the night before, she lay curled into the blankets, her head on the pillow he'd used.

For the first time, he felt something different for her. He didn't want to take her; he wanted to protect her, wrap her tighter in those blankets, pull her into him, and keep her from what she was about to be thrust into-his family problems-Lycan problems.

Ares slid down the doorjamb to the floor and watched her. For more than an hour, he took in the rise and fall of her chest and the sound of her light snores.

RIVER

RIVER SNUGGLED INTO THE BLANKETS AND PILLOW THAT SMELLED OF Ares. Her hips ached from sleeping on the floor, but it didn't deter her from refusing to move. His scent soothed her wolf and her as well. She didn't know how she felt about that.

Her stomach growled. What time was it? Definitely early morning since not a speck of light peeked into the room yet. Her stomach growled again. Dang. If she got up, would anyone notice? Was there anyone still in the suite? There had to be at least someone, but where did they sleep? She hoped they didn't sleep on the couch. That wouldn't be fair. Ares' bodyguards needed sleep. Did they take shifts? So many unanswered questions.

River stretched as the ache in her stomach grew worse. She couldn't sleep until she'd eaten. Pulling one of the blankets closer around herself, she stood. As she drew closer to the door, she stopped. The door was open, but she had shut it. As her eyes adjusted to the darkness, she recognized the outline of someone sitting in the doorway's threshold, their back against the door jamb and their legs outstretched.

Lachlan? Or Zeke? A scent tickled her nose. *Ares.*

Why the hell was Ares sleeping in the doorway? Her heart squeezed. She didn't want to wake him, but she didn’t want him to spend the night sitting either. She chewed her lip, then crossed to him and shook his shoulder.

"Ares."

His eyes flew open, and he stood before she blinked. He scanned the room, then his gaze landed on her, and his posture relaxed.

"Are you all right?" he asked.

"I'm fine. I just… Sleeping like that didn't look comfortable, so I wanted to…" To what? Did she want to invite him in? To tell him to leave? She had no idea.

"I'm sorry I woke you," he said. "I didn't mean to."

She shook her head. "It wasn't you. I wanted something to eat."

"You're hungry? What do you want? I can wake my chef and-"

"No. No. Please don't. I don't need anything fancy. I didn't eat much at dinner, so I thought I'd grab a snack."

He nodded. "We always keep the kitchen stocked."

River brushed the hair from her face and tried to flatten it as she followed him down the hall and through the dining area. Ares flipped on the light in the kitchen, and River looked into the living room, happy not to find any of the bodyguards there. A door on the other side of the living room opened, and Theo walked out.

"Need anything, Boss?"

Ares shook his head. "We're fine, thanks. Go back to bed. We have an early morning."

Theo nodded and closed the door again.

"You don't need to help me if you have an early morning," said River. "I can find something."

Ares opened the cupboards. "We have ramen, cereal, crappy canned spaghetti, and crackers." He opened the next one. "Or, if you want something better, we have microwave popcorn, coffee, hot chocolate, mac and cheese, soup, and..." He pulled out a small jar and showed it to her. "Caviar?"

River couldn't help but chuckle. "Wow, that's quite the variety."

"You'd think a group of college guys lived here from the cabinet stock."

"Now I see why you have a chef."

He nodded and put the jar back. "Let me check the fridge."

"That's okay, I'll do the popcorn."

"You have to eat more than popcorn."

"I will at breakfast, but that'll hold me."

He looked like he might argue, but instead, he nodded, pulled out a bag of microwave popcorn, and tossed it in the microwave.

As the microwave did its thing, the two looked at each other. The air between them grew uncomfortable, and River glanced away.

"So... why did you sleep in the doorway?"

"I didn't mean to. I only... came to check on you."

He wasn't saying something, but she refused to pry.

The popcorn beeped, and Ares pulled it from the microwave and poured it into a bowl.

He prodded the bowl toward her. "Do you want a drink?"

She nodded and popped a handful of popcorn in her mouth.

He opened the fridge.

"Soda, please."

"What kind?"

"Whatever."

He pulled a soda and a beer from the fridge and handed her the soda.

"Do you like those?" she asked.

Ares inspected the beer. "Not particularly."

"Then why do you drink it?"

He regarded her for a moment.

"What I mean is, most humans drink them to get buzzed or drunk, but a shifter has to drink a ton of them to do that, and I assume a Lycan would have to drink even more. So, why drink it if you don't like the taste?"

He set the beer on the counter. "Honestly, I have no idea."

She chuckled as he opened the fridge and pulled out a sparkling water instead.

"Interesting choice."

Ares' eyebrows slammed together. "Why?"

"You don't seem like a sparkling water guy."

"I don't like plain water, and soda is too sweet, but I like the carbonation and fruit flavor, so…"

Something about his choice intrigued her.

She shoved more popcorn into her mouth. "Beach or woods?

He sipped his bottle of water and then cocked his head to the side in such a cute way it made River want to kiss his nose.

Where the hell had that come from?

"Would you rather go to the beach or camp in the woods?" she said.

"Uh… beach? What about you?"

"The beach, because I've never been before. But I do sunburn easily, so maybe not."

"I'll make sure you are covered from head to toe in sunscreen," he said.

Thoughts of Ares' skilled hands rubbing lotion all over her body made her tingle. She took a long swig of her soda as her cheeks heated.

"Play or movie?" she asked.

A slight smile played across his lips. "Play. I love the theater. What about you?"

"I'd have to say movie because I've never been to a play."

"But you live in New York."

"I haven't taken the time to do things most people do since moving here. First school, then work, and making my art."

"If we were going to be in town longer, I'd take you to one."

River's stomach flipped at the thought of leaving in a few days to return to Ares' compound. Leaving her life and everything in it.

"We'll go next time we are in town," he said. "I'll check my calendar. When I travel back, we'll go to two or three."

She threw him a smile. When? A month? Six? She picked at the popcorn.

"Renaissance or modern art?" he asked.

His question caught her by surprise. "Well, that's a tricky one. My favorite is DaVinci, but I am also a huge Dali fan. I happen to be a huge fan of Tim Burton as well. And Hayao Miyazaki."

"Burton isn't an artist."

"Isn't he? Have you seen his work? It's incredible. Only an artist could have made *A Nightmare Before Christmas*."

Ares nodded. "Agreed."

"What about you?"

"Honestly, I don't know much about contemporary artists."

"Well, we'll have to remedy that. You can take me to the theater, and I'll take you to my favorite art museums."

Ares smiled. "It's a date."

"Okay. When?"

"When what?"

"When can we do it?"

"Uh… Well, I need to-"

"Check your calendar to find out when we are coming back. Right. I forgot."

Ares' mouth opened and closed again.

Damn, River. Why do you have to be such a bitch?

"I should head to bed." Ares gulped down his water and tossed the bottle into the trash with the beer he didn't open.

"Ares?" River said as he walked away.

He stopped but didn't turn back.

"I'm sorry," she said. "I…I don't mean to be like this. I don't, I just… This is all so much."

Ares sucked in a breath and strode back to her. Quick but gentle, he raked his hands into her hair and kissed her. It wasn't forceful. It wasn't needy. Just a soft caress of lips like a lover would give to his beloved. Then his lips planted on her forehead, and he kissed her a second time before he withdrew.

Without a word, he turned and left. River's wolf whined at the loss, and River shivered as goosebumps pebbled her skin. As she stared at the spot he'd stood moments before, she wanted nothing more than for him to come back and kiss her again.

CHAPTER TEN

ARES

It'd been three days since Ares had seen River, but every night when he returned to the hotel, her fragrance had lingered in the corridor between their suites, causing his wolf to grow increasingly more agitated.

Zeke and Theo had kept him apprised of her every move. She'd stayed in the hotel. Gone to her workshop to finish a project. She'd met with her mom and Strider for lunch, and they brought her two duffle bags of things for her. Bianca had stopped by almost every day. But she hadn't come to him. Not once.

On the third night, Ares' wolf couldn't handle being cooped up so close to her and not in the same room. To touch and taste her. He'd been forced to cut his last meeting short due to his complete lack of control and had returned to take a cold shower and have a few rounds with his hand. But neither did anything to quench his wolf's frustration.

Around eleven p.m., he called for Theo and Santiago. He'd dressed in a tight black T-shirt and pair of jeans and walked into the hall. He stomped to the elevator and poked the button.

"Where do you want to go, Boss?" asked Santiago.

"Out."

"Anywhere specific?"

The bell on the elevator rang, and a light laugh pierced him straight in the heart. The doors opened, and River stopped laughing. Bianca, Zeke's mate, let out a small squeak, noticing the men.

Ares' wolf roared to life, but he fought the beast back into its cage.

He stepped to the side, and Bianca moved around him, heading for River's suite. River stepped out, her eyes raking up and down his body.

"Hi," she said, her voice husky.

Ares nodded. "Beloved."

She choked down a lump, and they stared at each other for several moments.

"Are you prepared to leave?"

She licked her lips and nodded.

"The car will be here at nine a.m. to pick you up and take you to the plane."

Her eyebrows scrunched together. "Are you not coming?"

"I'm going to take a later flight. I have a few meetings left. But Lachlan and Zeke will make sure you arrive safely."

"Oh."

He wanted nothing more than to hold her. To crush her into his body. To take in her heavenly aroma and rub it all over himself.

The elevator doors began to shut. He reached out to stop them and nodded for Santiago and Theo to get in. He entered the elevator, and Theo hit the button for the lobby.

"Where are you going?" River blurted. "I didn't think you went to meetings so casually dressed."

"I'm not going to a meeting." He wanted to ask her to join him, but didn't. Mostly because he didn't think he could take her rejection.

The doors slid closed, and as they did, she said, "Bye."

Ares shut his eyes and reclined against the wall of the elevator. His wolf told him to go up and talk to her. Nothing about her demeanor had tried to shut him down.

Instead, he walked into the lobby.

"Where to?" Santiago asked again.

"A club. Any club. Just make sure it's loud and crowded."

CHAPTER ELEVEN

RIVER

The elevator doors closed, and River's wolf whined.

Ares' cologne lingered, making her body heat with desire. The past days without him had almost been unbearable. Her heart and mind had battled minute by minute as to whether she should go to him. Everything mixed inside her.

Her body and wolf wanted Ares. Wanted to feel his skin and taste his breath. But she couldn't trust the parts of her that wanted to explore every muscular inch of his form. An even more imposing and deliciously sexy form in his tight T-shirt and jeans.

His temper knew no bounds, and when he lost it, she couldn't help the terror that made her worry he might strike her or, worse, take her against her will.

"Are you okay?" Lachlan asked from the door of the suite.

She turned to him. "Where did Ares go?"

"Uh… I'm not sure, to be honest."

"He wasn't dressed like he usually is for meetings."

"He doesn't have a meeting tonight. They finished earlier this evening."

River bit the inside of her lip. "He said he is leaving on a later flight than we are."

Lachlan nodded. "He has some meetings to finish up, Highness."

River sighed. "How many times have I told you not to call me that?"

"Thirty-six, Highness."

River snorted and momentarily glanced back at the elevator.

"Are you hungry?"

River shook her head. "No thanks."

Over the past few days, she'd gotten to know Lachlan, Isaac, and Zeke. Lachlan had played cards with her and taught her about the ways of the Lycans. Isaac had told her about the estate and what Montreal had to offer. Both had been her constant shadows, though somehow, in their presence, she'd been more comfortable than with Ares. Even so, despite being hot and huge, there wasn't one ounce of attraction to either of them.

Ares. Ares mate.

Yeah. I know.

They walked into the suite to find Zeke talking in hushed tones to Bianca. They stopped when Zeke spotted her. Bianca scowled, and Zeke sighed.

"What's going on?" she asked.

Bianca opened her mouth, but Zeke answered. "We're discussing the plan for your departure in the morning."

Bianca stared daggers into the back of Zeke's head and opened her mouth again to say something.

"Bianca," said Zeke. "You might want to start organizing the things delivered to our suite. Now would be the time."

She stood and huffed. He reached for her hand, but she whipped out of his grasp and bared her teeth. Zeke didn't so much as blink at her outburst. Something was up.

"I need River's help," she said.

Zeke looked between them as if trying to decide what to do.

"Prince Ares did say I, his beloved, could go where I wanted, didn't he?" River pressed, making sure to extenuate the word Prince.

Zeke's jaw worked hard for a moment. "He did."

"Lovely." Bianca gave a sardonic smile as she linked arms with River. "Then we will be on our way."

She turned, pulling River back to the suite door. Lachlan ran after them and got to the door first, pulling it open for them.

"Wait," said Zeke.

Bianca paused.

"I'll go with you," Zeke finished.

"Well, if you are going, I don't want to stay here alone," said Lachlan.

"Hey," Isaac interjected. "I'm right here, dude."

Lachlan snorted.

"Wonderful," said Bianca. "Looks like it's a party."

THE GROUP WENT DOWN ONE FLOOR, WITH BIANCA AND ZEKE refusing to look at each other. It wasn't until they entered the master suite that Bianca let loose.

"What is going on with you two?" River asked.

Bianca stormed over to River. "He doesn't want me to tell you."

"Tell me what?"

"Ares went out."

"And?" She drew out the word while waiting for the answer. "What, is he with a hooker or something?" she joked.

"No," said Bianca. "But he might as well be."

All blood drained from River as a chill swept over her. "Where is he?"

"Clubbing."

River's wolf roared to life at the thought of other women pawing at Ares. Her Ares. She envisioned him grinding up behind them. His firm hands roamed their bodies. His lips on their skin.

Without warning, a growl escaped River as a possessiveness overtook her senses.

"Where?" she roared.

TWENTY MINUTES LATER, RIVER AND BIANCA LEFT HER ROOM dressed to conquer. When they approached the front room, Lachlan's mouth fell open, and Isaac turned and coughed as he choked on his drink.

"I want to go out," River announced.

The men stared at her as she placed her hands on her hips.

"Hellooooo?" said Bianca. "Did you hear River? She said she wants to go out."

"Dressed… dressed like… like that?" asked Isaac.

"Is there something wrong with my outfit?" River looked down at the black leather bustier and mini skirt covering most of her assets.

"Uh…" The men shared a look.

"Zeke went to grab some food. He'll be back any minute. We should wait for him," said Lachlan.

"I don't want to wait," said River.

"But it's for your safety, Highness. If anything happened to you, Prince Ares would have our heads."

"Do you know where he is?" River asked.

"Who?"

"Ares?"

"Not exactly."

"Well, find out and take me there. Surely you can't get into trouble if you take me to him. He did say to watch me only if I wasn't with him."

The men exchanged another look, and Isaac shrugged.

LACHLAN STOPPED THE SEDAN OUTSIDE THE CLUB WHERE RIVER HAD first met Ares. She jumped from the backseat, her wolf a bundle of nerves. She couldn't settle between anxiety and complete rage.

River strode with Bianca to the rope, and Frank turned their direction.

"Damn, River," he said with a huge smile.

River smiled as he opened the rope and let her in. "I've been told Prince Ares is here."

Frank snorted. "Oh, he's in there all right. Why? You looking to get with a Lycan? In that outfit, I'm sure you're bound to grab the attention of every male in the place."

River started for the door. "That's what I plan on doing."

Bianca ran to catch up with River as she entered the club and scanned the surroundings. She sniffed the air, searching for the scent she wanted.

Weaving through the bodies, she hardly noticed the catcalls, whistles, and 'hot damns' aimed their direction.

She scanned the dance floor, and a male stepped in front of her. Blocking her view. He placed his hand on her bare hip.

"Why don't you let me buy you a drink or ten, pretty mama?"

River glared at him. "Why don't you remove your hand before I break it?"

"Come on, babe. You can't come walking into a place like this, dressed like that, and expect to-"

River's wolf lashed out. She gripped the shifter's hand and twisted until his wrist cracked.

He cried out, and she bent into his ear. "I warned you."

She turned to the bar and ordered Bianca a soda from Jimmy.

"I'm sure Zeke will be here any second."

Bianca nodded, and a shifter smiled at her.

Uh… nope.

River spotted Isaac. "Take her to the VIP area and keep her there. Soda only or water until Zeke arrives."

Isaac nodded and took Bianca's soda before helping her through the crowd.

When they disappeared, River scoured the floor. In the middle, Ares danced, surrounded by four human females grinding on him and touching him all over.

River's wolf snarled as Ares moved in ways that would have made the Magic Mike dancers envious.

Minutes passed with her anger rising to a level she'd never known. Suddenly, his eyes popped open and trained right on her. They shifted from his normal color to golden and back again as his mouth fell open slightly.

He stopped moving as she descended the steps, raking over her body. Good. First mission accomplished. She'd gotten his attention. She squeezed through the throng of patrons and beelined straight for him, realizing that she hadn't thought of anything beyond getting his attention. He watched her with the fiery gaze of a predator.

River's wolf snarled, and she shoved the first female off him without even looking at her. The girl cried out and stumbled to the ground.

"What do you think you're doing?" asked another female, helping the first off the floor.

The two women advanced on her, but River leveled her gaze on them.

"Back off, this one is taken." Every instinct inside her wanted to carve into their faces and gouge out their eyes for daring to admire Ares. Let alone touch him. He belonged to her and her alone, and River wasn't about to share.

The girls backed into the crowd. River spun around and glared at the other two women, who backed off as well.

Breathing heavily, she trained her gaze on Ares. He didn't move for a moment, but then he reached for her. She swatted his hand away.

His eyes went black, and they continued to stare at each other, fighting for dominance. His aura pulsed around her, pushing her to look away, to submit, but she refused.

Finally, he stepped so close their bodies brushed against each other, and he slipped his bare arm around her hips, pulling her against his bulging erection.

"You're lucky I haven't ripped the heads off every male in this place for daring to look at you or smell you," he said in her ear.

"And you're lucky I don't chop your hands off for touching those whores," she retorted.

He backed up a pace, but she fisted his T-shirt in her hand and yanked him back to her. "I didn't dismiss you."

He ground his hips into hers. "If it makes you feel any better, I only thought of you."

She leaned in an inch from his lips. "If you're going to lie to me, keep your mouth shut." Then she turned her back to him and pulled his hands to her hips. A rumble escaped him, and he ground into her harder. As she flung her arms around his neck, he bent down and inhaled her, sending shivers over her skin.

RIVER WASN'T SURE HOW LONG THEY DANCED BEFORE ARES ushered her off the floor toward the VIP area. All she knew was she should never have gone clubbing in leather, and she never would again. The bustier made her itch, and the skirt clung to her thighs.

Santiago stepped aside and let them through, without looking at River.

Ares dragged her through the booths, past where Zeke and Bianca locked lips in a tangle of limbs, to the back of the room where Drew sat on a couch with a leggy brunette.

Drew jumped to his feet the moment he spotted them and ushered the female from the room.

The instant they reached the back, Ares' mouth clamped down on hers, but she shoved away from him.

"Sit," she commanded.

Like an obedient dog, he sat, his greedy eyes taking her in.

"What the hell are you playing at?" she demanded.

"Me?" he asked, wide-eyed. "I'm not the one who came out in public dressed like that."

"And I'm not the one found being fondled by human skanks."

His nostrils flared.

"Say something," she said.

"Something."

She growled and stepped toward him.

He held up his hands. "All right. All right. Fine. The truth is, I didn't think you'd care."

She blinked. "I'm sorry?"

"You've made it clear you don't want this mating, and I needed to blow off some energy to keep my wolf from-"

Her wolf snarled at the idea of him with another female.

"From what?"

"From forcing me to come find you and be near you."

“Are you saying it's my fault you went out and let other women be all over you?"

He didn't reply.

"Fine. I guess you won't mind if I go blow off some energy by letting guys caress me all over."

She didn't make it one step before he blocked her way, growling.

"So, it does matter."

"Only if you want to avoid a massacre."

"Why is it any different for you?"

He licked his lips. "I suppose it's not. But what if I went out there dressed in only underwear?"

"This isn't underwear."

He cocked an eyebrow.

River folded her arms over her breasts. "I wanted your attention."

"Oh, you got it, Sweetheart. The question is, what do you want to do with it?"

Her body heated. What did she want to do with it? The way he eyed her like he wanted to devour her tempted her to say something flippant or sexy. Instead, she said, "I… I like what we did before."

"Dancing?"

She nodded.

His arm snaked around her, and he kissed below her ear, sending goosebumps up her arms. "Then let's do that, Little Wolf."

CHAPTER TWELVE

ARES

The moment Ares spotted River across the room wearing barely anything, he was gone. The women grinding against him were little better than mutts compared to the goddess who would be his mate.

Seeing her toss the girl off him had almost sent him over the edge. The fire in her eyes said everything. He was hers, and she wouldn't let anyone else have him.

His wolf had howled and ignored everyone else in the club.

His mate. His Omega.

They spent the rest of the night pressed against each other, dancing.

By two a.m., the club had started to wind down, and they had gotten into the car together, heading back to the hotel. Wrapping his arms all the way around her, he realized how fragile she felt. It amazed him that such a small little wolf could be so fierce- like a little fluffy Pomeranian.

Ares chuckled.

"What's so funny?" she asked between yawns.

"You're small but so feisty. Like a Pomeranian."

She yawned again. "As the daughter of the pack's enforcer, I was constantly challenged by those who wanted to show me up or wanted to threaten my mom."

Ares' eye twitched. "You were beaten?"

"Not much. As I told you before, my bite is worse than my bark."

Ares laid his chin on her hair. "You tell me who they are, and I'll rip their teeth and claws out individually."

He waited for her to respond, only to be met by the steady beat of her heart and a light snore.

CHAPTER THIRTEEN

RIVER

River awoke the next day to the fragrance of flowers. She sat up on the bed to find she was still in her outfit from the night before. Ares' side of the bed hadn't been disturbed.

Her wolf whined. He hadn't stayed with her.

They'd made headway last night. Somehow, in the hours of dancing, she'd let go of everything that plagued them and just was. He was a terrific dancer, of course, as if he would be anything else with a body like his. And in those hours, touching and holding onto him, she'd been more intimate with him than she ever had with the guys she'd slept with. And in that intimacy, something had clicked for her. Something she'd been trying to deny since meeting him. They were mates.

She pulled her hair. A mate. She had a mate. A hot, rich, royal mate. What the hell did she do with a mate- besides the obvious? She didn't want to be a princess. She didn't want to have servants and bodyguards. She wanted to make her art and... be normal. But normal had gone out the door the moment she was born. Only she'd not known it until a few years ago.

Even then, she'd thought she would be okay if she took the pills, used the sprays, and stayed away from shifters for the most part. But here she was with the fated mate of all fated mates.

She swallowed. Ares had been in the room, and he hadn't stayed. From what she remembered, he hadn't tried anything. He'd not even taken her clothes off her.

Every movement when they'd danced, he'd let her lead. If he touched her, it was because she'd wanted him to. On the ride to the hotel, he'd done nothing more than hold her. He hadn't tried to kiss her or anything. He'd been a perfect gentleman. Something she'd not thought he would be.

She scolded herself. Why had she thought that? Because of what she'd been taught about Lycans growing up, which made her as ignorant about supes as humans.

The aroma of flowers struck her again, and she walked to the bright bouquet of irises, lilies, and peonies sitting on the table. She sniffed them, and her body flushed with heat. She couldn't help the rush of joy that trickled through her. A man had never bought her flowers before. Maybe being mated to a prince wouldn't be so bad. Not if he would buy her flowers.

Her wolf chuffed. She glimpsed a card and removed it from the vase.

Beloved River,

I cordially invite you to an evening of food and culture.

I will be back to pick you up at four.

Yours Truly,

A.

Something about his romantic gesture lifted her lips into a smile. She never thought she'd be the kind of woman to be wooed with flowers and the promise of expensive food, but apparently, she was.

She chewed the inside of her cheek, remembering Ares' kiss from days before.

Wait. She was supposed to leave for Canada. Had he changed his mind? Could she stay a few more days? A few more days… with him?

She reread the card. Maybe being mated to the hottest man on Earth wasn't the end of the world.

River did something she'd never done before. She went to an actual hair salon and got her hair washed, cut, and styled. It'd always been an extravagance she'd never wanted to splurge on before, but for some reason, she wanted to impress Ares. They were fated mates, which meant he was supposed to love her if she looked like she'd romped in a bale of hay and showered in mud, right? Even so, she wanted him to like what he saw when he saw her.

A thrill raced through her as the hairstylist spun her around to see her reflection. Damn! She had no idea her hair could do that. It'd been twisted, braided, poofed, sprayed, and teased into a design River had a hard time figuring out where it began or ended.

"Do you like it?" The hairdresser beamed.

"Absolutely. Thank you, it's… incredible."

He smiled so brightly River thought his face might crack.

Theo stood and walked to her. "Done?"

River nodded. "Do… do you think Ares will like it?" Her stomach tied in a knot. Stupid. She sounded like a stupid, silly girl with a crush.

Theo gave her a genuine smile. "He will love it, Princess."

The idea warmed River and made her wolf yip.

Okay, calm down, it's just hair.

Her wolf would not be deterred from happiness. She made her pleasure at River's trying to impress Ares clear.

Lachlan went to the counter and placed four-hundred-dollar bills down. Outside, Zeke waited at the corner of the building, and Theo showed her to the sedan and opened the door.

The hairdressers gawked at the window and talked animatedly to each other. She wondered if she'd ever grow used to the attention that came with all the money and influence Ares had. She sure hoped not. She didn't want to be one of those women. She wanted to stay who she was. Grassroots. Down to Earth. Not extravagant. But it wasn't every day a woman met her fated mate, and he took her on a fancy date. So this once, she would deal with the stares and whispers and relish being pampered.

RIVER HADN'T PLANNED ON GETTING MORE THAN HER HAIR DONE, but moments after she returned to the car, her phone buzzed with a text telling her she had an appointment. Confused, she stared at the text until Lachlan pulled up to a day spa. River glanced up in confusion as Theo opened her door for her.

"What are we doing here?" she asked.

His brows furrowed. "Didn't you get the text? You have an appointment."

"For what?"

"Ares said it's for whatever you want."

"I...uh..." Her cheeks heated. She'd never had a massage before, and somehow, having someone else massage her body seemed wrong. Not just that, her wolf would be too irritated to enjoy it. "I'm good. Can we go back to the suite?"

Theo glanced at his phone and back at River. "Don't you want to… you know, do all the stuff they do at spas?"

River snorted, easing her tension. "Theo, we haven't known each other long, but do I seem like the kind of girl who likes spa stuff?"

His eyebrows rose, and a smile crossed his face for the first time since she'd met him. "To be honest, no. But Ares wants you to be happy."

"Taking me to the spa isn't quite my idea of something that would make me happy."

Theo nodded. "I understand, but…"

"Say what you have to say."

He looked at her hard for a moment. "I'm mated, and there isn't anything I wouldn't do for my mate. In the beginning, I knew nothing about her. I bought her all kinds of stuff to make her happy. She accepted all of it and acted like she loved every single thing because she wanted me to be happy. As we got to know each other, we no longer needed to try so hard. We learned what it took to make the other happy. But initially, I wanted to show her I wanted nothing more than her happiness. I did a lot of things and gave her many things I thought would make her happy. In return, she appreciated my effort, even if it wasn't what she wanted."

River thought for a moment. "Are you asking me to go in there and do spa stuff because it will make Ares happy?"

He nodded. "He is trying. This fated mate thing is awkward and tough and not something you want, but it won't go away between you. I wouldn't be his friend if I didn't ask you to please give him a chance. He wants to make you happy. Knowing you enjoyed yourself will do that for him."

River choked down the sharp retort on her tongue and pressed her nails into her palms. After all, wasn't that what she'd decided to do after seeing the flowers? To give him a chance? Isn't that what she wanted? She liked the flowers. So, didn't it make sense she'd want to do something for him?

River inspected her hands. "I guess my nails could use attention, and I've never had a pedicure."

Theo helped her from the back of the sedan.

"Thank you."

She had no idea how to respond. How did one respond to a man who thanked you for getting your fingernails painted?

River had never been so nervous, and she had no idea why. She sat on the bed in her hotel room and fiddled with her hair as the minutes ticked by. She watched the clock. Four fifteen. Had Ares changed his mind?

She felt like a high school girl waiting for her prom date. At least her nails were perfect. The ladies in the salon had removed all the oil and dirt under her nails, filed them into cute little round nubs, and painted them clear. She'd not been able to do that since starting art school.

The front door to the suite opened, and she peered at the suite door. Drew entered first, followed by Ares talking on his phone. Santiago walked in last.

River didn't know who Ares talked to, but his raised voice and agitated posture said something wasn't right. She wondered if their date would be canceled, but as he spoke, he turned and spotted her.

He stopped speaking, and his body relaxed.

Her heart thundered as their eyes connected, and neither moved.

He was power personified. Sex on two legs. Even from yards away, his Alpha presence called to her Omega side, and she couldn't deny the tug which propelled her to him.

Santiago and Drew disappeared as Ares shoved his phone in his pocket, and without another word, they gravitated toward each other. He stopped a foot from her and took her in from head to toe before closing the distance between them and folding her into his muscular arms. He buried his nose in her hair and inhaled. His familiar cologne and something metallic washed over her, and she relaxed.

How did the simple feel of his body pressed against hers and his scent filling her nose soothe her?

As she went to wrap her arms around him, he kissed her head and backed away.

"You're like… like an angel sent from the Luna Goddess."

River chuckled. "No one has ever called me an angel before."

Ares smiled, but his eyes looked troubled. She wanted to reach for him and smooth the lines that creased his forehead.

"I'm sorry I'm late," he said.

"Did your meetings go well?" she asked.

He licked his lips. "Not exactly."

A pit formed in her stomach. "If you don't want to go out or have other meetings, we don't have to."

Ares took her hand. "Absolutely not. There will always be more meetings, but I won't let them interfere with my more important duties."

"More important duties?"

"As your mate."

The sincerity in his words and earnestness in his voice made her heart squeeze.

"Let me change, then we can go." He turned to leave, but she clutched his hand, and he turned back.

"I like what you're wearing now."

He smiled. "I'll be right back."

She didn't know what else to say.

Ares kissed her knuckles and walked to the door. Santiago and Drew followed him out, and Theo shut the door with an expression of something she couldn't fully read. Appreciation?

As soon as Ares left, recognition dawned on River. The other smell; the metallic one on Ares.

Blood. It was blood.

ARES

ARES GINGERLY TOOK OFF HIS SUIT COAT AND WALKED INTO THE bathroom with Santiago, who carried a first aid kit.

He pulled his dress shirt from where it clung to his stab wound. He turned sideways. It had been significantly deeper when it had occurred an hour earlier, but now was little more than a gash.

"I told you I'm fine," Ares said to Santiago. "You're such a mother hen sometimes."

"Better a mother hen than a Lycan without a king."

Ares and Santiago looked at each other momentarily, and Ares nodded.

"What about you? How is your wound?"

Santiago shrugged off his coat and pulled down the collar of his dress shirt. "Already healed."

Ares nodded. He hadn't expected the trouble with the pack of rogues living on the city's fringes. He'd not known they'd been residing near New York, and he wondered if one had bitten his River.

He walked to the sink, found a washcloth, and dabbed his wound.

He'd spent over a year looking for the one responsible for trying to organize the rogues. He'd heard the wolf had traveled to the States, but as of yet, he'd been unable to find him. It was only a matter of time, though. Ares would find the wolf responsible and kill him. More than ever, he had to squash the rogue uprising. Now that he had River, everything had changed. He would be crowned king, but more than that, he now had something to lose. His Omega.

Santiago laid his hand on Ares' shoulder. "We'll find him and end him."

Ares nodded and bandaged his wound before grabbing a new shirt and pulling it on. All thoughts of the traitor gone, his mind moved on to far better things. Things like seeing River waiting for him. He'd barely registered the voice talking in his ear as he spotted her. Hair up, make-up on- though she didn't need any- she'd been gorgeous in the silvery-colored dress he'd picked to match her hair. She'd been more than stunning; she'd been breathtaking. It'd taken everything he had not to rush to her and take her straight to the bedroom. But he'd remembered her eyes when he'd kissed her before. He'd never seen them like that. Open, vulnerable, inviting. It'd been that image he'd clung to. That memory, which had kept his wolf in check and had forced him against all instinct to pull her softly to him. Merely seeing her face and catching her perfume had soothed him in a way he'd never experienced.

He snapped on his cufflinks, and his phone rang. The name "Pompous Asshole" appeared on the screen. He snarled and rejected the call. He was done with assholes for the day. For the next eight hours, he planned to focus on one person and one person only- His Omega.

CHAPTER FOURTEEN

RIVER

River and Ares sat at a small candle-lit table in the Guggenheim Museum, surrounded by Van Gogh. She took a bite of her steak and stared at the *Montagnes à Saint-Rémy*.

"I'm sorry they don't have any Davinci," Ares said.

River tore her eyes from the beautiful painting of the Alpilles mountains to see if he was joking. He swirled a glass of dark *Cabernet Sauvignon,* as the label read, and took a sip.

"You're serious."

"You said he was your favorite."

She snorted and nodded. "Yes, I think he's a genius, but you realize we are sitting at a table in the Guggenheim Museum, drinking what I can only assume is expensive wine and enjoying artwork by Vincent Van Gogh, right? The Vincent Van Gogh. That's not anything I thought I would do in my life."

"So, you like Van Gogh?"

How did she answer that question? "You see that painting?"

"The mountain one?"

She nodded. "Van Gogh painted for ten years before he sold one piece of artwork. He painted that in a mental institution. A mental institution! And then killed himself later that year."

"Wow, you're doing much better than he did. You sold out your first show."

She scoffed. "Because you bought everything."

He smiled. "If I hadn't, someone else would have."

She regarded him for a long minute. "Why did you buy all my pieces? To impress me?"

He swirled his wine again, watching it. "Not impress per se. More to get your attention."

"And did you think I'd want all my pieces going to one place, or did you think it would have made me happier knowing they stood all over the place so more people might enjoy them?"

He lifted his gaze. "Do you want me to give them back to the gallery?"

Her gut clenched. Did she?

"Did you even like any of them?"

His gaze intensified. "I loved all of them."

"What do you like about them?" she tested.

He didn't answer immediately, and she feared he was lying to her.

"I loved the flow of them. The gentleness yet strength. They are like you. Beautiful and delicate but rigid as steel."

River's throat dried, and she lifted her wine and gulped. No one had ever said anything like that about her work before. Even the people at the exhibit said they were amazing. Beautiful.

Expertly crafted. But none had seen them as representations of herself.

She smiled, glad he'd bought them all.

"Why are you smiling?" he asked.

Her cheeks heated. "I… I'm glad you bought my sculptures."

He lifted an eyebrow. "You are?"

She nodded.

"Is it because as soon as we are mated, what is mine is yours, so you'll have them back?" He grinned.

"What? No. I didn't realize that."

His smile broadened. She liked how his smile lit up his dark eyes and mellowed them.

He set down his glass of wine and checked his watch. "We only have about another hour."

She nodded and finished her wine before standing.

Ares rushed around the table and pulled her chair out for her.

She turned to face him. "You don't have to do that."

His eyes grew serious. "When you enter the room, everyone will stand. When you exit, they will stand. No one will eat until you've taken a bite. No one will sit before you have been seated. And I will always, always pull out your chair for you and push it in for you. You are my Omega. You will only ever be treated with the utmost respect. If you aren't, the punishments will be dire. Even to myself."

River opened her mouth, but once again, he'd left her speechless. So, instead, she approached him, reached up on her toes, and kissed his cheek.

Ares pushed her chair into the table and offered her his arm. When she linked it with his, he winced. The memory of the odor of blood when he'd picked her up bubbled to the surface, and she pulled to a halt.

"What's wrong?" he asked.

"Were you hurt today?"

His gaze flickered for a moment, and then he smiled. "I'm fine." He took her arm, but she slipped it away.

"That's not what I asked," she pressed.

"It's nothing. I'll be healed by tomorrow morning at the latest." He moved to retake her arm, but she backed away a step.

"Show me."

"River, it's nothing. Let's enjoy the museum on our own while we can."

Anger boiled inside River, and she stepped up to Ares. "You say I am your Omega. You say I am not to be disrespected. The biggest form of disrespect in my book is dishonesty if you want me to respect you. To trust you. To… love you… you need to do the same. If you want me as your Omega and your mate, I say okay. But if I do, I'm all in. Everything. Between you and me, there can be no secrets. You need to share with me. Everything. The good, the bad, the awful. Can you do that?"

A fire sparked in Ares' eyes. "Yes," he said in a husky voice.

She searched his eyes for deceit, but there wasn't any. "Let me see."

He didn't move. "And what about you? Will you go all in? No secrets? Share everything? The good, the bad, the awful?"

River's heart thundered, but she didn't look away. "Yes."

She thought he might kiss her again as heat swirled around them and the air sizzled with tension. She wasn't sure what had happened, but something changed between them. Like a tumbler in a lock, a piece clicked into place.

Ares unbuttoned his suit jacket and untucked his shirt. He

turned and lifted the tails of his shirt, showing her a bandage between six and eight inches long.

Her gut clenched, and her wolf whined. Someone had hurt him. Hurt him bad. Her Alpha. Her mate. Anger crashed through River, and when their eyes met, she was all too aware that her claws and teeth had lengthened.

A tender smile played on Ares' lips, and he tucked in his shirt.

"Your anger touches me more than words can say, Little Wolf. But it will take more than a fight with a couple of rogues to take me from you." He brushed his lips across hers, but when he moved to pull away, she fisted her hand in his shirt and pulled him to her.

He brushed his knuckles over her cheek, but didn't deepen the kiss. He broke his lips from hers a moment later and took her hand.

"Come on. We haven't seen the sculptures yet."

Body shaking, wolf howling, River let Ares usher her out of the room to the next exhibit. Her mind whirled, unable to comprehend what was happening between them… but her wolf sure as hell did. Little by little, though they hardly knew each other, she and Ares were becoming mates.

ARES

ARES LET RIVER LEAD HIM FROM SCULPTURE TO SCULPTURE FOR AN hour, talking about the artists, the medium, and the techniques. Though he'd never remember a fraction of what she told him, his wolf chuffed with happiness to be with her and listen to her so passionate about something. Listening to her talk about art brought out a different side of her. The beautifully vulnerable little wolf she'd buried under piles and gallons of descenting spray, blocker pills, and pain.

On their way to the opera, the Director of the Guggenheim texted Ares to make sure everything had gone well. Ares thanked him for opening the museum to them, which was normally closed on Tuesdays, and promised another sizeable check. One of the perks of being heir to the Lycan throne and a sizable fortune was knowing many influential people. It also helped when those people were supernaturals, either loyal or afraid of him.

"So where are we going next?" asked River.

"We did something you loved, so now I'm going to take you to something I love."

"The theater?"

Having someone remember the personal things he said had never made him happy before, not that he talked about himself much. With River, everything was different. Everything was heightened, more intense, and more meaningful.

"To the opera."

"What play?"

"Carmen. It's not in English, but it'll have subtitles above the stage. If you get lost, I can explain it to you. It's quite simple. A harlot seduces a young soldier and ends up destroying his life."

"That's your favorite opera?"

"To be honest, most of my favorites seem sad, but to me, Carmen is something I've always wanted."

"To be destroyed by a woman?"

"Exactly. To love a woman so much, nothing else matters to me but her. A woman I would give up everything for. A woman who makes me lose all sense of reason. A fated mate."

Her cheeks flushed.

The car stopped. Theo opened his door, and Ares exited. He buttoned his suit jacket as he sniffed and scanned the crowd for danger, but Santiago, Drew, and Lachlan were already on it. They positioned themselves casually but strategically up the wide staircase and then nodded to Theo.

"We're good."

Ares turned and helped River from the car. She stopped momentarily as she took in the thick crowd and sniffed the air. Her eyes darted around and landed on Lachlan up the steps, and her shoulders relaxed a fraction.

Ares held back a growl at the thought she might have feelings for Lachlan. Of course, she didn't. She was his mate. His. He wanted her to be comfortable with his men. They were, after all, her men, too. The more relaxed she became with them, the more comfortable she'd be in his world.

Ares kissed her head. "Come on, Little Wolf."

They walked together to the steps, where she gripped his arm for support. The small gesture made his wolf sigh in contentment. Ares wrapped an arm around her and steadied her. Halfway up the staircase, Ares began purring, and by the top, he purred so loudly his body practically vibrated.

River stopped and placed her hand over his heart. "What is that? I've never heard anything like it before."

Ares stopped. "I… uh… I don't know how to explain it. It's like purring, I suppose. I've never done it before."

She didn't remove her hand. Her thin fingers rubbed the fabric of his jacket.

"It's so… comforting. Is it an Alpha thing?"

"Honestly," he said. "I have no clue."

They stared at each other as if in their own bubble of warmth. Eventually, she removed her hand and turned to the door.

"We should go so we aren't late."

Ares nodded, and they continued inside.

RIVER

ARES LED RIVER TO A CENTER SEAT ABOVE THE ORCHESTRA LEVEL. All around her, the sound echoed, and people laughed and smiled, excited about the performance.

She moved her knees in as Lachlan sat on the other side of her, and Theo sat next to Ares. She didn't know where Santiago and Drew had gone, but figured they couldn't be too far away. She wondered if Ares' bodyguards liked opera and art museums as well. She couldn't imagine following someone around day in and day out and hating where they went.

She turned to Lachlan, who scanned the crowd ever alert. "Have you seen this one before?"

Lachlan smiled. "Many times, Highness."

"Lachlan, you can call me River."

His gaze traveled to Ares, and he shook his head. "I wouldn't dare, Highness."

River looked at Ares. "Seriously? You called me that before I met Ares."

Ares gave her an impassive expression. "That was before."

Her lips twisted. "What are people supposed to call me?"

"Her Highness. Omega. Princess. And when you are my mate, you will be called High Luna or Her Majesty."

"But never by my actual name? The one given to me by my dad?"

"Your birth name is only for your closest family and friends."

"And you want me to trust my bodyguards, right?"

Ares' eye twitched. "They will call you Highness, Omega, Princess, High Luna, or Her Majesty."

River clenched her jaw. "Theo calls you Ares."

"Theo has been my brother since childhood. Zeke's mate Bianca may call you River. Your mother and stepfather may call you River. I may call you River."

"What about Zeke? He'll be my brother-in-law."

The lights dimmed, and Ares didn't answer.

River huffed. She didn't want to be called any of those things. She wanted to be called by her name. She liked her name. Her father had given it to her. He'd said when she was born and opened her eyes for the first time, they reminded him of the river by their house.

River bit her tongue and turned to the stage as the orchestra began to play. This wasn't the end of the discussion. Not by a mile.

CHAPTER FIFTEEN

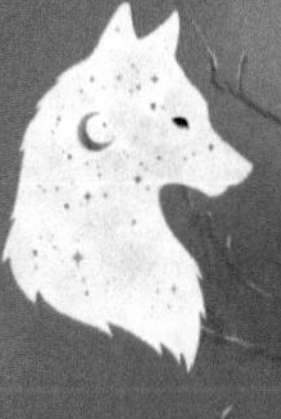

RIVER

"What did you think?" Ares asked as they walked down the stairs to the exit of the opera house.

"I enjoyed it more than I had anticipated. The music was beautiful. The sets and costumes were incredible. I can hardly believe all the work that went into the production. I thought it would be like watching a movie, but somehow so much… more. I can't explain it."

Ares smiled at her. "Exactly."

River caught the whiff of a familiar scent, and a chill settled over her. To her left, a man bumped her on the stairs, and a stinging sensation pricked the back of her hand.

She lurched forward in her heels. Ares grabbed her in a flash and had her steadied before the thought of falling occurred to her.

"Hey!" Ares boomed.

Theo grabbed for the man's jacket, but he rushed through the crowd down to the landing and onward.

River's mind caught up with her body, and a surge of adrenaline crested through her. That scent. She would never forget it.

Him.

River shook and bent over the railing, looking for the man who had bumped her. Again, she glimpsed a black jacket rushing down a floor below.

"Are you all right?" Ares sniffed and lifted her hand. "You're bleeding."

River peered down at it. He'd scratched her hand, and a light line of blood welled on her skin. She tried to find words as Ares searched her face.

"What is it? Are you ill?"

Her throat dried, and she tried to form words. "It's him," she managed.

Ares looked at her for a moment, confused.

She touched her neck.

Ares' eyes turned to fire. "Theo! Zeke. Bring me that Lycan's head."

Theo and Zeke shot down the stairs without a word.

Ares crushed her against him, and she clung to him, trying to force herself to calm down.

"I'll kill him, River. I promise. I'll kill him."

He was there… in New York. At the theater. It couldn't have been a coincidence. Was she overreacting? Maybe she was wrong. Perhaps it was someone who smelled similar.

Her wolf said one word. *Him.*

Ares growled. Two couples stopped on the stairs. Their eyes flashed red. Drew and Santiago formed a barricade between Ares and the couples, though a crowd of other people poured down the stairs between the two groups.

"I am Prince Ares Wolvenguard, and this is my Omega," Ares said in a voice so low River almost didn't hear it. "Keep moving," he commanded.

The group inclined their heads and continued down the stairs.

Vampires. She'd never seen vampires before. Or if she had, she'd never known it. Though she wasn't scared of them, it showed her how something as small as a scratch could cause unwanted attention from other supernaturals.

She'd never understood why Cherry and the others had always said living in a crowded city was dangerous. Humans weren't the only predators in the cities. While wolves tended to stick to the outskirts, many other supernatural species needed to be near for food, services, and business. But she'd seen more supes in the last two minutes than in the four years she'd been at school. Not that she'd searched. She'd refused to make friends at school.

Several males slowed their pace, but their human companions continued to move downward. The males' gazes landed on River, hungry and lusty. She pressed her head into Ares and turned her eyes away from them.

Damn! What? Was her blood magical or something? Why was she a beacon for supes?

"Move, or you'll lose your eyes," Ares snarled. "Your choice, pups."

River's heart thudded. She'd never experienced males looking at her before. Human men, sure. But shifters? Never. Mostly, they'd ignored her. She'd always thought it was because she couldn't shift-until the night she'd been attacked. Then she'd learned it was because of the pills her mom had made her take since she was twelve. The sensation left her feeling vulnerable for the first time, and she realized why Cherry had hidden the fact that she was an Omega.

"Let me help you," Lachlan said in a terrifying voice she'd not thought him capable of.

Lachlan unbuttoned his jacket, flashing a shoulder holster she didn't know he wore.

The shifters regarded Lachlan, then her, one more time. Lachlan took a step forward, and the males moved off.

Tension rippled through Ares' body. "I need to get you to my estate. They'll keep looking at you until we are mated. All of them. Shifters. Lycans. Vampires. Fae. Doesn't matter."

River looked up at him. "So, mating will make it stop?"

"No. You will always attract males. But once you are mated, they'll smell me as well, and they'll back off. Or they won't, and I'll kill them." Ares' eyes flashed golden.

River swallowed hard. She'd always felt in control. She could protect herself. But, in that moment, she realized how vulnerable she was. She didn't like it and wrapped her arms around Ares' waist.

"I want to leave," she whispered.

Ares nodded.

"If Theo and Zeke find the male, they'll call," said Santiago. "Let's take you back, Highnesses."

River looked down at the scratch on her hand. He'd attacked her. Again. Not like before, but… he'd been there, next to her. Though it had only been for a second, the thought terrified her. But another thought followed. Had he known where she was for the last four years?

Ares held her hand the rest of the way down to the front door and stopped. Outside, people raced away as rain sloshed down.

Only a few stragglers remained in the lobby, trying to order Ubers or find taxis without ruining their designer attire.

"Damn," said Ares. "I should have checked the weather. I'm sorry."

"There's an umbrella in the car, sir," said Lachlan.

Santiago nodded. "You and Drew drive up the car and bring the umbrella back for the Prince and Princess."

"No need," said River. "I may come off like the wicked witch sometimes, but I don't melt in water."

Ares cocked his head to the side. "I wouldn't call you the wicked witch."

Her eyebrows rose.

He shook his head. "Self-preservation and past traumatic experiences don't make you a witch. They make you tough, and having to be tough makes you cautious."

What the… How did he see her like that? She'd never thought of it before, but… he was right. She'd never had someone understand her before. Not that she'd ever given a guy a chance, but still… At that moment, she wanted nothing more than for Ares to be her mate.

Mine. My Alpha. My mate.

River nodded. *Ours. Our Alpha. Our Mate.*

A white ribbon appeared out of nowhere and wrapped around

her wolf's leg. Slow and silky like a lover's hand. It stopped at the ankle, and the rest lay next to her. River anticipated the panic. Waited for her wolf to freak out, but she didn't. She howled with delight.

River's heartbeat quickened, and she couldn't breathe.

"What is that?" she whispered.

Ares ran his fingers up her arm to her chin and tipped it upward. He met her lips with his in the most tender kiss she'd ever experienced.

"It's our bond," he whispered. "It's growing."

He kissed her again, and River's body heated with need. She wanted him right in the lobby of the opera house. She didn't care that people surrounded them. Didn't care that Theo, Zeke, and Drew were with them. Didn't care about anything or anyone else.

"Ares," she whispered, sliding her hands up his pecs.

"Yes, Beloved?"

"I-"

The door pulled open behind them, and the cold, wet air rushed in, making her tense. Lachlan stood outside, the umbrella open for them.

Ares exited, and wet droplets stained his jacket sleeve.

"Theo or Zeke should have called by now," said Santiago.

Ares looked at his phone. He'd had it on silent. Even so, it hadn't buzzed.

He pulled River to him. "Something doesn't feel right."

She wanted to say something more, but couldn't form words.

Lachlan moved in and held the umbrella over River and Ares' heads while he got soaked.

"This is silly," said River over the noise of the street. "Lachlan is drenched. You hold the umbrella and let him get in the car."

"I'm fine, Princess," said Lachlan.

River laid her hand on Ares' arm. "Ares, please?"

The thunder of rushing footsteps pulled her attention.

"Ares!" Theo yelled, coming around the corner of the building. "It's a trap!"

Ares roared, and Santiago moved to her side.

"Get her out of here!" Ares shouted.

Theo turned as two men emerged from the shadows, and he fired his gun. One of the men went down, but the other had only been struck in the shoulder. He roared and lumbered forward, his fangs lengthening along with his nails. His shirt shredded as he transformed on the steps of the opera house and sprang at Theo.

Ares roared and leaped the ten-yard distance between himself and Theo, snatched the wolf midair, and ripped its throat out.

River sucked in a breath, and Ares turned. "Go," he bellowed. Water poured down his body, thinning the blood and soaking his face and torso to a light pink.

Santiago took River's elbow and pulled her away. "Princess, we need to leave."

"No." She turned back to find a wolf on Ares' back. Three sprang out of the bushes. "You need to help him."

Santiago ushered her toward the car. "Sorry. My Alpha gave me a command."

"But-" River's words cut off as two wolves bounded toward them.

Santiago jumped in front of her and pulled his gun. He fired, but the first wolf dodged and kept coming.

Lachlan and Drew appeared out of nowhere and tackled the second wolf. The group slipped on the rain-soaked steps and tumbled down toward the street.

What the hell was going on?

The first wolf leapt at Santiago, but River grabbed a knife from her thigh and flung it at the shifter, hitting him square in the eye.

Santiago turned to her, and she rushed down the steps to the wolf's body and pulled her blade from him before wiping it on his fur.

"Damn, rogues. Where's your master?" She kicked him hard in the face. "Where is the bastard? Tell me!"

The rogue was dead. Damn. She should have aimed lower.

Santiago reached her and pulled her away from the animal. "Let's go."

"No! We need to help Ares." She pulled away. Ares and the others fought a pack of no less than six rogues.

Her wolf roared. Her mate. They attacked her mate.

Santiago yanked open the car door. "Princess, please!"

"We have to go back!"

Santiago shook his head. "Please. Ares can handle himself. If anything happened to you, *that* would kill him. And in turn, he would kill me. Please. I promise he will be fine. If you're here, he won't be able to fight effectively."

Reluctantly, she slipped into the front seat before he slammed the door and rushed to the driver's side.

Her wolf howled and thrashed, wanting to help Ares.

No! This is the best way we can help him right now.

Her wolf disagreed.

Out the window, Zeke ran into view, a gun in each hand. He fired at three emerging wolves. Ares moved like a blur, grabbing and tearing the wolves apart.

How the hell would they explain to human officials?

Santiago put the car in gear and tore out onto the street to the sound of screeching brakes and honking horns.

River craned her neck to see the fight, but she couldn't make anything out but blurs between the rain and the other cars.

River's gut clenched. *Dear Goddess. Please watch over him. I don't want to lose him. Not now.*

Blood soaked the knife in her hand. If she ever found the Lycan who'd bitten her, she'd kill him herself.

CHAPTER SIXTEEN

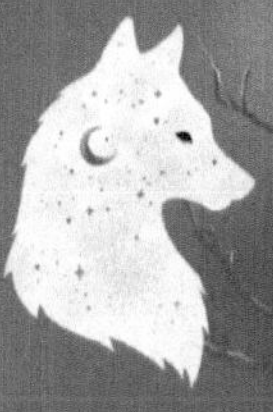

RIVER

River paced the suite.

"Please sit," said Bianca. "You're making me want to throw up."

River stopped in front of the blazing fireplace. Her little sister hugged herself.

"I'm sorry." She sat next to Bianca and put her arm around her.

River had no doubt Ares could handle himself, but Zeke and the others were something else. She'd never seen them fight, and as hybrids, she didn't know the extent of their strength. But they were Ares bodyguards, so they had to be capable, right?

"Zeke still hasn't called me. Do you think he's okay?"

River hugged her sister tight. "He's fine. They both are." She said the words mechanically, unsure whether or not she believed them. She'd know if something happened to Ares, right? Her wolf would know.

Not necessarily, she realized. He'd been stabbed earlier, and she hadn't realized it. The thought pushed River almost to the point of hysteria.

Santiago's phone buzzed, and then River's.

We're on our way up. It wasn't from Ares number.

"They're back." Santiago went to the door to wait.

Bianca searched her phone. "I... I didn't get a text. Why didn't I get a text?" she pleaded with River.

"It's okay," said River. "Maybe he sent it when he got in the elevator, and there wasn't a signal." She bit the inside of her cheek. Ares hadn't sent the text either.

The bell rang, announcing the elevator, and Bianca rushed to the suite door.

"Ezekiel," she cried.

River stood and held her breath. Please don't let anything have happened to any of them.

A crash sounded as the front door banged against the wall, and a gigantic bloody mess in a ripped, expensive suit raced in. His black eyes scoured the room and landed on her by the fireplace. He stalked to her. Watery blood dripped off him and onto the carpet, staining it. He stared at her for a minute and fell to his knees, wrapping his arms around her.

"Beloved," he whispered into her stomach.

Relief flooded River, and a small cry flew from her lips. She pressed his head into her body and raked her fingers down his back.

"Ares."

A purr started and spread over her, making her fear drift away.

Behind him, the others strode through the door. Lachlan sported a bruise above one eye and a cut on his neck. Drew walked in drenched but seemingly uninjured. Theo entered next, unharmed, though covered in blood. He talked on the phone with someone, trying to calm them. His mate River assumed.

Theo spotted her and nodded before heading into one of the spare bedrooms to continue his conversation.

Where were Bianca and Zeke?

Finally, they walked in, Zeke leaning on Bianca heavily and holding his side. Bianca cried and fawned over him.

"You two take the spare room," River said.

Zeke nodded, and they headed toward the other room.

Ares' eyes were still black as coal. "I thought I would lose you."

"Why? You were the one attacked. All I did was get in the car and drive away."

He shook his head. "They were after you. *He* was after you."

"You… found him?"

"We made one of his rogues talk. He's been watching you."

She fought the fear coursing through her. "But it's been over four years. Why now?"

"He heard I'd found my mate, and she was an Omega."

River got the feeling he wasn't telling her everything.

Ares stood and cupped her face. "We need to fly back to my estate immediately and-"

"But you still have meetings," said Drew.

"Cancel them."

"No," she said. "This proves you need these meetings. If someone is willing to attack you in public…"

"She's right," said Drew. "If you go now, it will appear like you're running, that you are scared. It will give the rogue the excuse he's been looking for to gather more support against you. She needs to be at your side. They need to see her. Know she is real. A shifter

Omega is your mate. It will help sway them to learn your fated mate is a shifter, not a Lycan."

So, now she'd become arm candy? River thought about it, remembering how desperate her wolf had been minutes ago, thinking something had happened to Ares. If being with him might stop that from potentially happening again…

"I'll do it," she said. "If it will help. I'll do it."

"No. I won't take you to all the packs. That's too many chances something will go wrong."

"Bring them here," she said. "All at once. An area meeting. A dinner."

Ares growled. "This is my space. Your space. I don't want them up here."

"Downstairs. In the ballroom. We can have the hotel cater and organize everything."

"It's a sound idea," said Santiago. "We know the layout. It's your hotel. It will be like being on our own land. It will be easier to keep secure because we can station everyone at the exits. We decide the time, and we leave whenever you are ready. If things seem off, we come right up here and lockdown."

Ares licked his lips. "Have Vanessa arrange it for tomorrow night. I want out of here the next day."

River's chest squeezed. The next day? "I… can't we stay until the end of the week? I still have some things I want from my studio."

"I'll make you a studio. Whatever you want, I'll buy it."

Again, with the money.

"I appreciate that, but there are tools I'm used to. They're like an extension of my limbs. It would take me a year to break in new ones."

"Fine. I'll send Vanessa to make sure the whole thing is packed up and shipped to the estate."

River's wolf snarled, and River growled. "I don't want her in my space or near my things."

Ares nodded.

"I'll do it," offered Bianca as she and Zeke re-entered the room.

"B, I can't ask you to do that."

"You didn't ask. I'll go tomorrow, and you can Skype me to tell me what you want packed. I'll make sure it's done."

"But you have your things to pack."

"It can wait. I'm not leaving for a week."

River wanted to protest, but she'd be outvoted by, well, everyone.

"All right."

"Good," said Ares. "There's just one thing."

"What?"

"I don't want you at the meeting. It's too dangerous. There will be unmated Alphas, and even if I bring in all my men, I can't promise it will be enough to keep them from trying to get at you."

"So, you don't want me there?"

"It's not about want, Beloved. It's about keeping you safe until we are mated."

River wasn't a porcelain doll. She didn't need to be locked up in a cupboard and kept safe. Even so, the look in Ares' eyes told her he would not be swayed.

"All right." River took his hand. "Let's clean up."

He nodded and told his men to clean up, eat, and rest. Theo offered to be the liaison between Vanessa and Ares about the dinner, and Ares agreed, but said he wanted to pick the menu.

Then, before he figured out more work to do, River pulled him into the bedroom suite. She locked the door and then marched him into the bathroom.

ARES

Ares stared in the mirror. It'd been a long time since he'd been in a full-out battle, and what bothered him most was that his suit wasn't salvageable. Damn. He'd only worn it once.

"Show me your wound."

"I wasn't injured."

River cocked an eyebrow. "The one from earlier."

"River-"

"I wasn't asking."

Her expression told him she wouldn't take no for an answer. Damn, he loved the fiery protective side of her.

He licked his lips and undid his tie, dropping it to the ground. Then he took off his jacket as well. She watched him intently as he unbuttoned his shirt.

Without a word, she stepped to him and ran her hands over his skin, making him harden instantly. Her slender but strong fingers ran over his torso, his arms, and his back, checking for wounds. She lifted his arm and inspected his bandaged side.

She peeled back the tape and gauze. "You ripped it open. The bandages are soaked through. I'll clean it, and then we can rebandage it."

"River, there's no need."

She steeled her gaze. "I will clean it, and we'll rebandage it."

His wolf chuffed at her tenacity. Damn, he liked her.

"Then I'm looking you over and making sure you aren't injured."

She glared at him. "You know I wasn't."

"Why is blood on your dress?"

She inspected the dress. "Damn. I thought I'd been careful. I liked this dress."

"I'll have another one here in the morning."

"That's not the point."

She ran the water, retrieved a soft hand towel, and wet it.

"So why is blood on your dress?" he asked again.

She turned off the faucet. "Because I threw a knife at one of the rogues, and when I removed it, I got his blood on me." She went to dab his wound, but he gripped her wrist.

"What?"

She looked at him. "What?"

Fear trickled through him. "Santiago, let you fight?"

Her brows furrowed, and she snorted. "Let me? No, he didn't *let me*. I chose to defend myself."

He studied her, both amazed and angered. He'd told her to leave, but she'd chosen to fight instead.

"What's the big deal? There were more of them than us. You and your boys may be tough, but I've had enough of being attacked by rogues." River slid her wrist from his hand and pressed the cooling cloth to his wound.

"Why did you have a knife on you?"

"I've always carried one. My mom made me start when I was twelve. She taught me how to use it and made sure I always had one. I thought it was because I couldn't access my wolf, but…"

"It was because you're an Omega."

"I believe so. I now think a lot of what she did was because I'm an Omega. Explains why she never made Bianca do the same things." She turned the sink back on and rinsed out the hand towel.

"What kinds of things?"

River turned back with the wet washcloth. "Self-defense. Knife training. Emergency procedures to sneak out of the territory undetected. Natural ways to mask my scent. Just stuff."

Why hadn't Cherry told River the truth? She had to know at some point, River would meet a mate. Or maybe she'd hoped it would never happen.

"You should probably shower, and then I can bandage you."

"What about you? Do you want a shower?" Ares couldn't believe he'd said the words.

She laid the towel on the counter and stopped. He was about to take back the question when she turned around and brushed her hair over her shoulder.

"Will you unzip me?"

Ares froze.

His wolf lurched to his feet. *Mine. Mate. Take her.*

Back off, Ares ordered. No way would he let his beast ruin the moment.

With shaking fingers, Ares slid the zipper down River's back to the waistband of her panties. She let the dress fall to the floor, revealing a lacy set of pink underwear and bra he'd bought her, as well as a black thigh holster with two thin blades strapped to it.

It was the hottest thing Ares had ever seen. The fabric of his pants groaned as they stretched against his erection.

River unbuckled her thigh holster and laid it on the counter before walking to the roomy shower, opening the door, and turning on the water.

Ares feared moving. Afraid if he did, he might lose control again.

He took in the beautiful, sculpted lines of River's back and legs. Her spine stood out a little more than it should. The first thing he'd do when he got her to Canada was put meat on her. Anything she wanted. Anything she needed. He would give her.

For a moment, he imagined her body rounding out with pregnancy. Her breasts heavier. Her hips wider. The thought had him wanting to plow into her and give her his knot and his seed.

River stepped under the spray, still in her underthings, and turned to Ares. "Are you coming?"

Much longer, and he would be.

Unable to form words, he nodded and shucked off his shoes, socks, and suit pants next to her dress.

He had a pep talk with his wolf and told him what he'd do if his wolf tried to get out. Then he joined her in the shower. As he closed the glass door, the shower fogged up. As sad as he was, he couldn't see her in the steam; he was also glad for it. Especially since the tent he pitched in his underwear was embarrassing.

Wow! He'd never been embarrassed before. Not of his physique.

River picked up a bottle of something and squeezed it into her palm. Without a word, she moved to him and raised her palms, letting the slick liquid slide down his torso. His nipples hardened instantly at her hands on his skin. He brushed the wet hair off her face and slid his hands down her arms to her hips, where he rested them.

She lathered the soap all over his torso, moving in slow, meticulous circles, up over his chest to his shoulders, down his arms to his hands. She lifted them one by one off her hips and slid her fingers between his, massaging the palms of his hands.

He wasn't sure how to process the intimate sensations running through him. He'd never let someone touch him the way he let her. Without thinking, he began to purr, and her strokes on his skin soon went from light to more intense as she explored every line of his torso. She spun him to the wall, and he braced himself on it as she poured more soap on his back and kneaded his muscles.

Holy Goddess! She kneaded the muscles of his back with long, strong fingers. Stronger than he thought possible for someone her size. She worked her way down to his wound, gently put soap on her hands, and cupped them with water. She let the water-soaked mixture pour over the edges of the wound, and Ares clenched his jaw at the searing pain. She did the same thing twice more and then let the shower rain water over it.

Ares stood with his fists lying on the wall of the shower, trying to work through the burn in his side, when River's hands slid inside the waistband of his underwear and cupped his rear. The sensation almost overpowered him as her soapy hands ran over his backside, slick and warm. His purr increased, and when she slipped her hand between his legs from behind, he almost exploded.

Ares spun around and cupped her face, kissing her hard. He claimed her mouth with his, and she didn't resist. He fisted his hands in her wet hair and pushed her against the wall, his thigh parting her slender legs. She moaned into his mouth, and her hands skimmed down the front of his underwear. She gripped him and squeezed, making him jerk in her grasp.

He broke the kiss and dipped his head to her shoulder, nipping lightly. "River..." His voice came out as a strangled whisper.

Her firm grip squeezed again, and she moved one hand down to cup his balls as the other stroked him.

"River." Her name seemed to be the only word his brain could manage. He licked her neck and throat as she stroked and cupped him, making the back of his thighs burn, and his hips buck against her.

He nibbled her neck and up to her mouth once more. Her scent of vanilla and cherries invaded him, and he rocked his hips in her grasp. He wanted her. Wanted to be inside her, to feel her surround him in her perfect silkiness. He moved one of his hands down and tweaked her nipple between his thumb and forefinger.

She moaned into his mouth and kissed him harder. He slid his hand further down her body until he reached her silky folds. He rubbed his thumb over her most tender spot, and she pulled her lips from his and tossed her head back on the wall.

"Ares."

That's it. That was his little wolf. Her eyelids dropped halfway as he slipped his fingers between her folds, rubbing from her nub downward through her folds again.

The desperation in her voice as she repeated his name almost had him crashing apart. She gripped him harder and squeezed his balls almost to the point of pain. Ares' orgasm built, and he locked his lips on hers again as he slid a finger inside her. She mewled, and he withdrew and plunged two fingers inside her.

Her breath came out in panting gasps as she stroked him harder and faster. Ares held them both up as he curled his fingers up to find the magic spot inside her while massaging her nub with the heel of his hand.

With every stroke of his fingers, her movements became more frantic, and when she cried out, her walls clamped down on his hand. She stroked him so tightly that he came as well. Their frenzied movements continued as they both worked through their orgasms. When they'd both finished, he kissed her again, and she lapped at his mouth greedily.

She slid her hands from his underwear and folded her arms around his neck. He pinned her to the wall and kissed her until both of them were breathless and panting. As they gulped in air, he held her against him.

Ours. Our Mate. Our Beloved. Our Omega.

CHAPTER SEVENTEEN

RIVER

Ares had dried River and himself off, and then she'd gone into the bedroom and found some dry underwear and a cami while he went to the closet.

Her mind whirled at what they'd done. Every inch of him was as hard and ripped as she'd imagined a Lycan to be. When he'd slipped a finger inside her, it had stretched her. Just one finger. She imagined what it would be like having other parts of him inside her. And if he knotted her… the thought scared her.

She'd had a few one-night stands in her life with humans. They weren't built anything like Ares.

Her wolf had wanted her to bite Ares so badly and make him hers, but in the heat of the shower, River hadn't been able to concentrate enough to be able to. Thank the Goddess.

She met him back in the bathroom, where she re-wrapped his

wound, then picked up all the bloody things and piled them in the corner.

When she finished, she walked out to the bed where Ares sat on the edge, hiding something behind his back.

"Come here."

She did as he asked, but paused instead of sitting.

He patted the bed. "I promise I'm not going to bite." He smiled.

"Then what are you going to do?" She narrowed her eyes as he continued to smile.

She gave in and sat next to him. He turned her away from him, and the first tug pulled the ends of her hair.

He was brushing her hair. No one had ever done that before except Bianca.

"Ares, you don't have to."

He bent and nipped her shoulder. "And you didn't have to wash me in the shower."

Fair enough.

They sat in silence, and the magnitude of the day pressed down on her shoulders. He'd found her. Her attacker had found her, but not only found her, he'd known where she lived all along. But Ares had saved her. Santiago had saved her. Lachlan and the others had saved her as well. River couldn't wait to go to Canada if it meant she'd be safer from her would-be attacker. She had to be safer there, didn't she?

"Ares?"

He kissed her shoulder. "I won't let him near you again. I vow it on my life."

Her chest squeezed, and she lay against his hard body and breathed him in. He wrapped his arms around her torso and pulled her against him for a long minute.

"For the first time tonight, I felt something I'd not felt since being bitten. And something I never want to do again."

"What, Beloved?"

"Vulnerable and weak."

"You are neither, and as my mate, I will make sure it never happens again."

She peeked up at him. "But I didn't feel it only for myself. I felt it for you as well. I wanted to stay and help you. Protect you. But I couldn't."

He stared down at her. "I love that you wanted to protect me, but that's my job. To protect you. I failed you tonight. It won't happen again."

He kissed her and then resumed brushing her hair. They sat in silence for several minutes, but the silence wasn't tense or uncomfortable- it was peaceful.

"Coffee or tea?" Ares asked.

"What?"

"Do you prefer coffee or tea?"

"Soda."

He chuckled.

"What about you?"

"Water."

She smiled. "Sweet or savory?"

His breath caressed her skin. "I always like a little bite with my sweetness." He playfully nipped her shoulder, sending sparks shooting straight to her core.

Mate. Alpha. Mine.

She turned over her shoulder and brushed her lips against his. His tongue swept into her mouth, and she turned around and reached for him, but he pulled away.

She lifted her eyebrows.

He turned her back around. "As much as I'd love to, I'm only halfway done with your hair."

River wanted to protest, but if she didn't get her hair brushed, she might as well shave her head in the morning. It would be a thousand times easier.

As he began detangling the next section of hair, she relaxed.

"Movies or books?" she asked.

"I prefer books, but rarely have time to read anymore. I do listen to audiobooks, though. What about you?"

"I prefer movies. Books are awesome, but like you said, there is not much time for reading."

"I can give you access to my audio library," he offered. "I listen to the books at about two times the normal speed and can finish two on a long plane flight."

"Impressive."

He moved on to the last section of her hair.

"So, what was your favorite class in college?" he asked.

"I liked art history a lot. Learning about different masters, periods, movements, and everything else. What about you?"

"I don't know that I had a favorite class. I took what was required to graduate."

"You didn't take any classes for fun?"

"Didn't want to waste the time."

Her gut clenched. "That's so sad."

"My parents made it clear I was there to be educated. So that's what I did."

"Did you have friends in college?" she asked.

"Did you?"

They were a lot more alike than she would have ever imagined.

He pulled her hair back, brushed through it one more time, and put down the brush. "Done."

River ran her fingers through her hair and smiled. "Thank you, Ares."

"My pleasure."

River yawned, and Ares lifted her to her feet and walked her to the side of the bed. He pulled down the sheets and tucked her in. He kissed her forehead and took a breath of her hair before standing.

"Goodnight, River."

River smiled at him, and as he walked toward the door, her smile turned to a frown. "You're leaving?"

Her wolf whined.

He stopped. "Do you want me to stay?"

Did she?

Yes, her wolf demanded.

"Do you mind?"

"Never."

Ares walked to the bed, pulled back the covers, and slid in behind her. She turned off the lamp, and he moved closer, setting his hand on her hip. River scooted back until his warm body spooned against her. He wrapped his arm around her, and she relaxed into him.

Mine. My Alpha. My mate. This time, it wasn't her wolf thinking it. It was her.

ARES

Ares awoke the next morning to find that River no longer curled next to him, but sometime during the night, she had turned over, and her body entwined with his. One of her legs lay between his, and her body pressed against him. Even one of her arms draped over his waist. He couldn't describe the sensation of having her so near. Her warm breath tickled his skin as he took in her scent.

He wanted nothing more than to lie with her forever, but he had work. He had to settle dinner so he could take her home and prepare for their mating ceremony with the council.

As he turned to roll out from under her, she murmured his name, and his wolf flipped over and begged for more.

Every idea flew from his mind, and everything he needed to do faded away as he pulled her closer and kissed her head.

Ares closed his eyes and savored her in his arms. He'd never slept in a bed with a woman before. Never held a woman through the night. Never awakened to her body tangled with his. And that was how he'd liked it until her. River had changed everything. He wanted her with him, on him, around him, every single second. The sensation was so foreign to him, but right at the same time. How had the feisty little wolf become such an essential part of his life in such a short time? And not only for his wolf but for him as well.

He relaxed back into her when a knock sounded on the bedroom door. He grumbled but didn't respond. Again, the knock sounded, and Ares' wolf snarled. If it weren't life or death, he would rip someone's head off for disturbing him and his mate.

Ares slid from under River's tangle of limbs, padded to the door, and opened it a crack. Theo stood waiting.

"What?" Ares barked.

"Sorry to bother you, Boss, but the caterer needs the menu for tonight so they can start prepping, or it won't be ready in time."

Ares groaned. He should have told Vanessa to handle it. No. He shouldn't have.

"Let me put something on."

Theo nodded, and Ares tiptoed toward the closet.

"Are you leaving?" River asked, not opening her eyes.

"I have some things to do before this evening."

She nodded. "I should get up, too. Bianca will be at my studio soon."

"I won't be long. If you need anything, Santiago and Drew are here. They can obtain anything you want or need."

"Can they get me you?"

Ares smiled and stepped toward her, but River made a soft noise that told him she was already falling back asleep.

When Ares walked out of his closet, River lay curled on his side of the bed with her face smooshed into his pillow. He smiled and wondered if she had consciously gone to his side of the bed or had done it in her sleep. He wanted to go to her and kiss her, but he didn't want to wake her again, so instead, he turned and quietly left the room.

Ares returned an hour later to River, standing with an iPad, talking into it and pointing things out to Bianca to pack up.

"Hey," he said.

She turned exasperatedly. "This is ridiculous. It would be much easier if I went to my studio and got the things I need."

Ares' wolf snarled, and he loosened his tie. "I have to finish the dinner plans, and I have a couple of meeting calls I need to make, so I can't. I'm sorry."

"I can go alone."

Ares growled.

"I didn't mean alone, alone. I meant with Lachlan and Theo. And everyone else, if you want."

"River-"

"Ares, you want to leave tomorrow, right?"

He clenched his jaw. "Yes."

"And you want me to be comfortable in my new home, right?"

Ares knew where the conversation was going and had no idea how to derail the train. He didn't want her out of his sight. He wanted her back at his estate. But he had a job to do and couldn't let an all-out war start because of his negligence.

"You can go. But you are taking Lachlan, Drew, Theo, and Santiago."

"Not Zeke and Isaac as well?" She smirked.

"Zeke is already there."

"Oh yeah. I forgot. While I'm out, can I-"

"No." Ares' voice came out stronger than he'd meant it to. "Your studio, and straight back. Too many Alphas are coming into town in the next few hours, and I don't want you out and about. And I had four more of my men come in early this morning. You will take them with you as well."

River's eyes narrowed, and to his surprise, she nodded. "Fine."

Ares blinked. "Fine?"

"Fine."

He studied her. "You aren't going to fight me?"

"Nope."

He didn't believe her.

She walked to him and touched his arm.

"What are you up to?" he asked.

"Nothing. You said no, and I said okay. That's all."

"Not with you, it isn't."

She reached up on her toes and kissed him. "Well, this time, it is. Maybe it's your Alpha charm working on me."

He snorted. "Yeah, right."

She laced her fingers in his hair and pulled his mouth to hers. Ares couldn't help but relax into her. Though his brain said she was up to something, the rest of his body couldn't care less.

"Honestly, the thought of all those Alphas being all over the place makes me nervous," she said. "Plus, having what? A dozen of your men with me doesn't make me want to go traipsing about town."

Ares cupped her cheek. "I won't let anyone hurt you."

She smiled. "I know."

He thought for a moment. "I should go with you. If there's any chance that… rogue knows where you are…"

"No. You need to do what you came for. I will be fine. If anything remotely seems off, I'll come straight back. Besides, they can park in the alley outside my shop door. There's no way in or out of the building besides my door. I've always been thorough about my security."

"If anything-"

"It won't."

He kissed her firmly as their tongues mingled. He pulled her closer, his body hardening at the memories of their shower the night before.

A knock sounded on the door, and River broke the kiss.

"What?" he called.

"Your phone meeting starts in five," called Theo.

"Coming."

He kissed River again, wondering if he would ever want to do anything but be in bed with her once they were mated.

"Do you promise not to do anything more than go to your studio and come back?" asked Ares.

River nodded. "Promise."

A memory stirred, and he narrowed his gaze.

"What?"

He let his erection press into her. "Don't bring any of the toys in your nightstand. You won't be needing them anymore."

River's mouth dropped open, and her cheeks flushed.

Ares smiled and pressed his lips to hers.

Before she said a word, he turned and left the room.

CHAPTER EIGHTEEN

RIVER

True to his word, Ares sent Theo, Santiago, Drew, and Lachlan with her to her studio as well as several newcomers whose names she couldn't remember. It was stupid, beyond stupid. But she didn't fight it because, surprisingly, it made her relax a fraction to have the men with her. Especially knowing her attacker knew where she might be. Hopefully, he wouldn't expect her to go home after being in the hotel for the week. Or better yet, hopefully, he'd gone back into hiding after the defeat.

In the past week or so, she'd been with them all, and she'd grown to like Ares' men. But more than that, she'd grown to trust them.

After packing up everything she wanted to take to Canada, she went to her bedroom and emptied her nightstand drawer into a trash bag. She'd been mortified Ares had found her little stash, but also aroused at the idea he would fulfill whatever she wanted from now on.

Now, sitting back in her room in the suite with Bianca, an assortment of room service meals sitting before her, she couldn't help but admit being away from Ares had caused an ache inside. He may have a million things going on, but she'd thought he might at least call or text her once during the afternoon. And when he hadn't, she'd found herself missing him.

"What do you want to watch this time?" Bianca asked.

"Something violent." River scanned the assortment of food and chose a fry.

"Really?" said Bianca. "I'd have thought after your night at the opera, you would want something tamer."

River snorted. "Like what? Hallmark?"

Bianca giggled.

The door to the bedroom opened, and Ares walked in. He noticed the half-dozen carts of food and then looked at River.

"Hungry?"

River huffed. "Yes. I just couldn't figure out what for."

He nodded. "I need to dress for the dinner meeting."

Bianca stood and crossed to the door. "I'll go check on Zeke."

Ares stepped to the side and let her go before closing the door behind himself.

River watched him for a moment, and he shucked off his coat. Tension surrounded him that hadn't been there when he'd left earlier.

"What's wrong?"

He turned. "Family stuff."

The words punched her in the gut. "Do you really want me to be your mate?"

He stopped and blinked. "How can you ask that?"

"I wonder because a mate is someone who is your equal. Your match. Someone you rely on and trust more than any other. And yet, it seems you aren't looking for a mate. You are looking for someone to keep your bed warm and do what you tell her."

His gaze narrowed. "You know that's not true."

"Do I? You've told me nothing about your business, your family, or what you know about the rogue looking for me. Am I gonna be like one of those mafia wives who is oblivious to what her husband does and instead is charged with running the household staff and changing diapers? Because I can tell you now, I'm about as domestic as a feral barn cat with rabies."

Ares burst out laughing, stopping River in her tracks. What the…? Was he laughing at her?

"Stop it," she demanded.

Ares laughed harder.

"I said, stop it. Stop laughing at me."

But he didn't stop. He tried, she had to give him that.

River stomped forward and smacked his chest. "Knock it off."

She went to slap him again, but he caught her wrist, and his eyes grew serious.

He pulled her against him and raked his fingers through her hair. "Yes, I want you as my mate. I just didn't want to lay everything on you at once for fear you might bolt again. The shifter world is a tentative place, but the Lycan world is different. It's ruthless and cruel." He studied her face for a moment, and his shoulders sagged. "The Lycan looking for you is my older half-brother, Titan. He wants you in hopes of grabbing the throne for himself."

His half-brother? The Lycan who had bitten her was Ares' older half-brother.

"Is that why you want me?" she asked. "So, you can secure the throne?"

Ares sighed. "When are you going to stop saying such foolish things? If you don't know why I want you and what I feel for you, I guess I'll have to prove it to you, Little Wolf."

River fought for something to say but couldn't form words.

Without a noise, Ares hefted her onto the table and spread her legs. River's body shook as he undid his belt and slipped off his shoes and tie.

River's body thrummed, and her wolf panted with need.

Him. She wanted him. Needed him. She needed to feel Ares, her Alpha, inside her.

River's g-string grew slick, and her body heated when his hand softly stroked her through the fabric of her pants.

Without realizing it, River bucked against Ares' teasing hand as he bowed his head closer and sniffed her.

A growl escaped him, and she yanked his mouth to hers. Ares grabbed her neck and pressed his body against hers.

River's wolf whimpered. *Mine. Mate. Alpha.*

River couldn't think. All day, her body had craved him. The things he'd done to her the night before hadn't sated her. It had made her needier. She couldn't explain it. She'd never been overly sexual before, but with Ares, every second they were together, the more she and her wolf craved him, wanted him, needed him.

She ran her fingers down to his waist and pulled his shirt from his pants before unbuttoning it and pushing it off him.

He ran a rough thumb over one of her breasts, and she couldn't hold back the moan that escaped her. She wanted him. She wanted him right on the table. In their bed. On the floor by the fireplace in the front room. She wanted him naked and hard inside her.

"I missed you today," he said.

"You didn't call or text or anything."

His lips found hers as she unzipped his pants, making him groan. "Did you want me to? I didn't want to bother you."

River looked at him thoughtfully. "I want you to bother me."

Their lips slammed against each other so hard their teeth clashed. He whipped her shirt over her head and kissed down her throat to the tops of her breasts.

"How much time do we have before dinner?" she panted.

Ares checked his watch and hissed. "Forty minutes."

She smiled. "We can do it in forty minutes, can't we?"

She went to pull his lips back to hers, but he froze.

"What's wrong?"

He stared at her, conflicted. "River, believe me when I say I don't want anything more than to make love to you right now, but I don't want to rush our first time."

"Forty minutes is rushing?" Damn!

He brushed the hair from her face and pressed his lips to her forehead. "It is with everything I want to do to you."

His words made her wolf mewl.

River tried to press her hand down the front of his pants, but he gripped her wrist and backed away. "If we start now, I will not stop for dinner."

"How can you tell me that and then leave me in this state? I think I will have to find one of those little friends of mine from my nightstand and give him a few rounds."

Ares threw his head back before looking at her again. "You are going to be the death of me, woman."

She chuckled, knowing he had no idea she'd thrown them all out hours earlier. "You better not die," she said. "I'd be lost without you."

Ares watched her without moving, and River wished she could take back the words. She'd basically told him she loved him and couldn't live without him. What the hell had she been thinking? She hadn't been thinking. Not with her head, at least. With her heart? Did she love him?

No. It wasn't possible. She couldn't love him. Like him? Yeah… sure… but love? No possible way.

Ares' eyes went black. "Do you mean it?"

River's throat dried. "I… I think I do," she stammered.

Surprisingly, he smiled. A genuine, whole-face smile which made his hard-angular face take on a softer, kinder appearance. He looked almost boyish, except for the eyes.

For a moment, she thought he might cry. Instead, he knelt in front of her and pulled her to him, laying his head on her breast.

River's heart clenched, and she ran her fingers through his hair.

She didn't know how long they sat, but when Ares rose again, another piece of their connection locked into place.

She touched his face. "I have something for you. I made you a present."

"You did?"

She smiled and pulled him toward the bed. She sat him down and walked to her purse. She came back with a small bag and held it out to him.

"What's this?" he asked.

"Something to wish you luck at your meeting."

He opened the bag and dumped two small pieces of metal into his palm.

A flutter of nervousness chilled her as he turned them over and revealed two steel wolf's head cufflinks.

He stared at them without speaking.

"You don't have to wear them," she said. "It's fine if you don't like them or don't have a shirt to wear them with or-"

Ares rose and grabbed her around the waist, pulling her to him. He cradled her head against his chest and breathed in her hair.

"I love you, River."

She blinked several times, then wrapped her arms around his waist and leaned into him.

"So, you like them?"

He inhaled her hair and crushed her tighter against him. "I love them too."

ARES

A PRESENT. RIVER HAD MADE HIM A PRESENT. NOTHING SHE could've done or said would ever mean as much in that moment as the knowledge that she'd thought of him throughout the day and had made something for him. He'd never be able to give her anything that would compare to what he felt for her and the tiny pieces of metal he clutched.

He couldn't believe he'd told her he loved her, but the words had tumbled from his mouth without a thought. Everything between them happened so fast that part of him couldn't believe it was real. But he'd spent his life hearing about the connection between a

Lycan and his mate from his parents. Even with them, the connection had paled against his feelings for River, his Omega.

River's breath came out as a hitched sigh, and she kissed him hard. His wolf howled pure and tender, calling to River's wolf. A sound that reverberated through him and echoed inside him.

River pulled away, and her eyebrows crushed together.

"What's wrong?"

"I… I… Did your wolf howl?"

Ares blinked several times. His wolf howled again.

River cocked her head to the side. "He did it again."

Ares' brain fought to understand. "You… you heard him?"

They stared at each other for a long minute.

"Can you hear my wolf?" she asked.

Ares shook his head. "What is she doing?"

River's cheeks flushed. "Uh, well, right now, she is on her back being a little tramp, so I guess it might be difficult."

Ares chuckled and sniffed River's throat. "I may not be able to hear her, but I can sure smell her." And damn if he didn't want to bury his face in River and taste every last centimeter of her.

He had no clue what was going on, but River was his mate, and as soon as this damned meeting was over, he would take her home, and he would never, could never, let her go.

CHAPTER NINETEEN

ARES

Ares had never wanted to run from anything in his life. But walking toward the ballroom full of Alphas, Betas, and more made him want to grab River, go straight to the airport, jump on his jet, and whisk her to the safety of his estate. But that wasn't an option. Not if he wanted to avoid making more enemies.

He took several breaths as he approached the ballroom. Two of his men who had flown in from his estate bowed to him and then grabbed the handles to the ballroom.

River was safe. She was upstairs. Up twenty floors. In his private suite. The floor wasn't accessible by anyone except him and his people. He had to focus. He needed to make this work with the shifters because if Titan had his eye set on the throne… the bloodshed would be overflowing. Ares needed everyone on his side.

Theo and Santiago flanked Ares, and the door to the ballroom opened. The scents of the different wolves struck Ares. Each wolf had their own unique aroma, tainted with adrenaline and their wolf's natural aggression. That's what happened when you had dozens of pack Alphas in the same room. Even so, his aura and command would make them kneel in his presence if he wanted. And he sure as hell did. He wanted nothing more than to command them into submission. But doing that wouldn't help the relationships between him and the packs.

All talking stopped as every head in the room swiveled toward him. He stood for a moment, allowing them to stare. He scanned the room and spotted Alphas he'd met before from different packs talking and drinking in groups. He made a mental note of who stood with whom, interested in which alliances had already been formed. He assumed most had been made through marriages and family bloodlines. A sizeable group of Betas from different packs stood on the other side of the room near the buffet table. An air of tension filled the space.

Theo stepped forward. "I present Prince Ares of Wolvenguard."

Without a word, each Alpha and Beta took a knee and bowed their heads. Again, Ares noted the ones slower to bow and those whose gazes didn't hit the floor. He would need Theo to investigate them as soon as they returned to the estate.

He didn't need to look at the other Alphas to know the things going through their minds.

"Here comes the New Lycan King."

"How did that monster score an Omega?"

"I'm going to rip his throat out one day."

Ares strode to the front of the room and prepared to speak when someone squeezed through the gathered group. Ares stiffened, and Theo and Santiago crossed in front of him as a small woman in a simple black halter dress with a long slit strode to the front of the room and stopped in front of Theo and Santiago.

She was pretty, with a light smattering of makeup. Older, in her forties. Her red hair piled up on her head, and stray wild curls framed her face, refusing to be tamed.

She snarled at Theo and Santiago in annoyance. "Where's my daughter?"

Holy shit. Cherry. He'd not recognized her all dressed up. He should have, though; only Cherry would dare to try and push past Alphas and Betas to find her daughter.

Ares decided he liked Cherry. She may be brash, irrational, and overbearing, but she loved River and would protect River with her own life. And he liked her for it.

Her gaze traveled to Ares, and he inclined his head to her.

"Cherry."

She inclined her head. "Prince Ares."

"My mate, River Whitetail of the Silver Moon clan, is in our penthouse. She preferred to stay somewhere more secure with so many unmated males here."

Cherry studied him for a moment as if deciding something, and then nodded. "Smart girl. I'll go to the penthouse then."

Ares nodded to Zeke. "Please take our mother-in-law to her daughters."

Zeke nodded, and Cherry followed him from the room. As if a colossal balloon had popped, the tension in the air deflated. The tall wolf, Strider, followed Cherry out of the room.

"Everyone eat, then we'll talk," Ares announced. And just like that, various Alphas and Betas moved to the buffet and picked up plates.

Many didn't move; they simply kept their eyes on Ares. Several moved to the open bar and ordered a drink. But the few younger, single Alphas worried Ares the most. Their jealous, angry gazes made Ares want to rip each of them apart.

Theo and Santiago moved behind Ares and took up their positions as sentinels.

As Ares did a full sweep of the room, he spied the last person he wanted to see. Vanessa. She stood in the corner by herself, staring straight at him. He signaled Santiago forward with a flick of his fingers. The hand signals he used with his guards had saved him on more than one occasion.

"Boss?"

"What's she doing here?"

Santiago followed Ares' gaze. "She said she wanted to make sure everything ran smoothly."

Ares gave a slight jerk of his head, and Santiago nodded and headed for Vanessa. She didn't wait for Santiago to reach her before she stalked to the door and out the exit.

Ares waited until everyone else had food before going to the buffet table. The room filled with the sounds of pleasure as the others ate, drank, and chatted. It made him smile. Shifters became much more amenable when they'd eaten a filling meal.

RIVER

Cherry's arrival did the opposite of making River calmer. She'd questioned River to no end about Ares and what he'd done to her. What she thought of being kept like a prisoner. How she planned on staying true to herself when he dictated everything she did. About leaving for Canada. About what had happened at the opera. And a million other things, setting River more on edge. Thankfully, Strider had realized River's waning patience and urged Cherry to return to the dinner after twenty minutes.

However, when two hours had passed and Ares hadn't returned, River wanted to rip her skin off.

"River, you can't." Bianca tugged on River's arm to stop her from going to the door.

"I can't stand it. I have to know what is happening."

"Princess, please," said Lachlan. "This is for your safety as well as Prince Ares'."

"I'm going crazy up here, not knowing what is happening." It surprised River as much as it did everyone else how concerned she was for Ares and the negotiations. She needed the shifter packs to back him. Needed them to believe in him. If they didn't… she didn't want to think about what would happen. If Titan wanted a war…

River marched to the door.

"Princess, I don't want to have to stop you."

River rounded on Lachlan. "How? You aren't allowed to touch me, are you?"

Lachlan ran his hand through his hair. "Well, uh… no."

"So, how will you stop me if you can't touch me?" She made for the door again, and as she reached for the handle, Lachlan stepped between her and the door and crossed his arms over his chest.

"Move." River's irritation rose.

Lachlan shook his head.

River tried to shove him out of the way, but he didn't budge. "Move, you giant lap dog."

Lachlan smiled. "Sorry. No can do."

River growled and pulled out her phone. She speed-dialed Ares' number. It rang twice and went to voicemail.

She dialed again. Again, it went to voicemail.

"Fine," River said. "If I can't go, let my sister out. Ares didn't say anything about Bianca having to stay in the room, right?"

Lachlan looked between them. "Well, no."

River prodded Bianca toward the door. "Go down and find out what is going on."

Bianca's eyes widened in horror. "Dressed like this?" She wore a lounge suit with the word 'cutie' on the butt.

"No one will see you. Peek in, see what is happening, and come right back."

Bianca scrunched up her face. "I don't think Zeke will like this..."

"It will be fine. He won't know. Please."

Bianca sighed. "Okay. But I'm only going for sixty seconds, and if I don't hear anything, I don't care. I'm coming right back up."

"Fine."

River nodded for Lachlan to open the door, and as he turned, River shoved him aside and slipped out the crack.

"Princess!" Lachlan called.

River punched the elevator button several times, and to her surprise, the door opened, and she ran smack into Ares.

Ares grabbed her by the arm, his eyes concerned. "What's wrong?"

She couldn't hold back the relief that flooded her. Her wolf chuffed with happiness.

"I... Nothing is wrong."

Ares' eyebrows creased. "You called twice in a row."

"I wanted to check on you." Her cheeks flushed with heat.

His gaze went to Lachlan. "I thought I told you to keep her safe."

"I'm sorry, Highness. I tried to-"

"Wait." River pulled her arm from Ares' grasp. "You told him to keep me safe, not prisoner."

"River-"

"Don't get mad at Lachlan; get mad at me."

The elevator dinged, and the doors tried to close. Ares stepped out of the way, and Theo and Santiago followed.

"I'm not mad," he said. "I'm concerned. There's a difference. Come on, I need to change anyway."

"Why? What's happening?"

Ares ushered her back into the suite, shucked off his coat, and undid his tie before they entered the bedroom.

"I am meeting a few senior Alphas for drinks."

"So, things didn't go well?" A knot formed in her stomach.

"No, things went better than expected. Even so, it won't hurt to recommit as many as possible. Some agreements need to be worked out."

"What kind of agreements?"

Ares slipped off his shoes and untucked his shirt before crossing to her and cupping her face. "Beloved, I will tell you everything I can later, but right now, I need to go. I wish I didn't, but it is what it is. This is my responsibility to all shifters and Lycans."

She wanted to protest and demand that he tell her what happened, but it would make no difference. He had responsibilities beyond his feelings and commitment to her.

She nodded. "I understand."

"You do?"

She crossed her arms. "Yeah, I do. I wouldn't say I like it, but I understand. I mean, I'm gonna have to get used to it, aren't I? Whether I like it or not, you aren't an everyday shifter. Or even a shifter Alpha. You're... well... you. And that means you have to take care of a lot of people. Like, a lot. I don't want to be the reason others are hurt. And if you don't do your job and get the Alphas on your side, people will definitely be hurt. So, do what you need to, and I'll wait for you."

Ares crossed to her, cupped her face, and clamped his lips down on hers. "I couldn't imagine anyone better for me than you." He laid his forehead on hers. "I honestly don't know how I survived before you."

River smiled. "Well, I know what I did before you. Whatever I wanted."

Ares slapped her rear. "Smart ass."

She growled. "Do it again."

Ares groaned. "River..."

"I know. I know. You have to go. But I need something from you."

"Anything."

"If I call, pick up. Tell me something, anything. Tell me you're busy. Tell me I'm annoying you. Tell me to strip naked and be ready for when you come home. Doesn't matter. Just... don't not answer."

She gripped his arms, hating how much she wanted him to stay with her.

A smile quirked up the corners of his mouth. "I think the last option is going to be a favorite of mine. I will probably use it quite frequently."

She laughed and unbuttoned his shirt, pushing it from his shoulders. "Don't be surprised if you receive the same message when you call me to find out what I'm up to." She undid his belt buckle and unzipped his pants. "Let's find you something more casual for your drinks."

Ares' stomach clenched as she raked her nails down his flesh.

"Damn, you make it hard to leave you, woman."

River glanced down. "I definitely do."

CHAPTER TWENTY

RIVER

Ares didn't return until almost four a.m. He fell into bed beside River, pulled her into him, and began to snore before she even asked how things went.

Four hours later, Ares awoke her, and they exited the suite and headed for the limos with everyone else. His warm hand on the small of her back comforted her more than she thought it could.

It didn't matter whether her feelings for him were because of the bond or because she was genuinely falling for him. All she knew was she'd never wanted to be with anyone else.

"So, when's the wedding?" Bianca asked. "You have to give me time because there's no way I am letting you plan this thing alone."

River laughed, and Ares pulled her closer.

"As soon as my mate wants the ceremony to be, it will be," he said. "After we talk to the council, of course."

Bianca wiggled her eyebrows. "The fall is a beautiful time to marry."

"That's two months away," said River. She didn't think she could wait two months to be Ares' mate.

"Why don't we wait until we're settled before starting the wedding plans," said Ares. "After all, you also have your own wedding to plan."

"Yeah," said Zeke. "You need to remember theirs isn't a simple shifter wedding. Ares is the Prince. That means many details have to be discussed and approved by the council."

"Approved?"

Ares shrugged. "It's nothing. They ensure all the right people are invited and things like that."

Somehow, River didn't think that was all the council would say about their wedding, but she decided to keep her worries to herself.

For the moment, her only thought was- she was getting married. Getting mated and married to the prince of the whole shifter Lycan world.

THEY LANDED IN MONTREAL AROUND ONE-THIRTY AND DROVE OVER an hour into a more rural area. On the plane, Ares filled her in on the previous night's events. A few smaller packs with younger Alphas weren't ready to commit to him. The older pack Alphas were on board, though. Surprisingly, her Alpha had helped sway a few undecideds to Ares' side of the fight. He'd also mentioned River being from his pack and how loyal Cherry and Strider were.

By the time they pulled up to an imposing gate, River couldn't believe how much the previous week had tired her. She'd barely gotten any sleep the night before, and to say plane rides weren't her favorite was an understatement. She'd never been on a plane before, and for being on one for the first time... well... she didn't want to do it again any time soon. Not to mention the tears and hugs with her mom, Strider, and Bianca, whom River reminded would be moving to the same place within the week. That, combined with everything that'd happened in the last two weeks, left her exhausted. All she wanted was a place for her and Ares to relax and breathe.

A guard in a little armored hut waved them through. Blue electricity zipped along the gate, and River hoped she never had to try to jump it to escape.

The car wound up a long driveway surrounded by trees and high walls, and Ares squeezed her hand. The sounds of wolves howling sounded all around the vehicle as they drove deeper into the estate. River's stomach clenched as they neared what would be her new home. The trees opened up into a clearing in front of a humongous house. She pressed her face to the window as it came into view.

"Holy crap!"

Ares chuckled, and his breath caressed her neck. "Welcome home, Beloved."

The limo stopped, and everyone piled out. The stone structure stood four stories high and as long as a football field. If they played hide and seek, she'd no doubt starve to death before being found.

The heavy wooden front door swung open, and several armed guards emerged onto the driveway.

Wow, how many bodyguards did Ares have?

"We can stay in the limo if you'd like, but I promise sleeping inside is much more comfortable," said Ares.

"Sorry. It's just so..."

"Amazing?"

River blushed, and he held open the door for her. Amazing wasn't the word for it. Opulent, grand, and too much were the words she would have chosen. But she assumed with him having to house all his guards and now his guards' mates, a sizeable estate was bound to be needed.

The fresh air invaded her as she stepped out. She closed her eyes and breathed in deeply. The only traces of pollution were the fumes from the cars. The scents of leaves, dirt, and flowers made her wolf jump up and whine. She wanted to be let out. She wanted to run.

All River had ever done was ignore her wolf, but now the grip was so tight she turned toward the edge of the clearing. Ares took her hand and pulled her from her thoughts.

"Not that way." He laughed and led her to the front marble steps. The new guards bowed.

"Highnesses," they murmured.

Ares nodded.

They entered the grand foyer, and River's eyes popped wide. Every surface of the entrance gleamed as if recently polished. Marble-tiled floors and huge paintings adorned the room. A chandelier with thousands of tiny crystals illuminated the space from high above. And to the left and right, two giant staircases wound upward and joined on the landing.

"This has to be a joke," she said.

"What do you mean?" Ares asked.

She snorted. "You did not grow up in this house. It's not possible. It's like living in a museum."

"And there's more than simply a foyer," Ares chided. "Come on. Wait until you see our rooms."

He pulled her up the staircase and headed down the left corridor. Everywhere she looked, a different piece of artwork hung. A tapestry, blown glass, or a sculpture or statue at least two centuries old. It might take River the rest of her life to be able to study everything in the mansion. Screw going to art museums, she'd stay home and study from now on.

They turned a corner and headed down another long corridor, past several heavyset doors. Several scents mingled together. Ares lived there, but... someone else did, too. Ares stopped before opening a heavy set of double doors. At the same moment, someone exited the room behind her.

A scent overpowered her. A trickle ran down her spine, and her wolf leapt to her feet. Ares continued into the room, but she couldn't hear what he said as a warm body approached her from behind. The aroma of wood and freshly turned earth permeated her nose, and her wolf howled.

Light fingers brushed the hair from her neck, and warm breath tickled her skin. A muscular arm snaked around her waist, and a low rumble sounded behind her.

"Mine."

River whirled around, staring into a set of bright hazel eyes. Her mouth fell open, and she blinked rapidly as confusion fuzzed her mind. She stared into the same face she'd seen for almost two weeks. Every inch identical to Ares, only... thinner, more angular. A small scar marred the brow above his left eye. He wore a soft but needy expression. A brown curl obscured one eye, and River reached out to push it away when someone ripped her out of the man's grasp. In an instant, Ares had the man pinned by the throat against the wall, teeth bared, eyes like midnight. The other man's eyes were equally dark, and he growled back and shoved Ares off him.

The two males circled each other until River wasn't sure who was who. One of the men lunged at the other and body-slammed him to the floor. They tumbled over and over, crashing into an end table and sending a vase shattering to the ground and flowers exploding everywhere.

Stop. Stop. Make them stop. River's wolf begged.

River stared on in horror, unable to move. Two of them. There were two. Twins.

Footsteps rounded the corner, and Santiago and Theo ran into view, followed by several guards she didn't recognize.

Snarls and slashing ensued between the twins. The smell of blood filled the air, and the sound of crushing bones. One kicked the other off, and he flew across the hall, crashing into a painting and sending it splintering to the floor.

"She's mine!" Ares bellowed, rushing the other man again. "How dare you touch her."

"You lying dog. She mine.” The other snarled as he met Ares halfway, and they toppled to the floor again.

"Not possible, you don't know her." Ares punched the man in the nose as his teeth elongated.

"Well, my wolf sure as hell does." The other man slashed Ares across the chest, painting his shirt with blood.

The guards rushed down the corridor and tackled the two bloodied men, tearing them apart.

"Ares!" Theo shouted. "Ares, stop!"

"Apollo," another guard shouted. "What happened? What's going on?"

Ares roared and fought against his guards, his nails lengthening and hair erupting from his arms. "I'll kill you this time. I swear I will."

"Not if I kill you first." The one named Apollo roared and fought his suppressors.

"Stop," said Theo. "Highnesses, please. Let's take a breath."

Both Ares and Apollo strained, ready to continue ripping each other to shreds.

"Ares, what is this about?" Theo asked.

Ares' gaze never left Apollo's face.

Then it happened. Theo let go for a split second, and Ares lunged for Apollo again. Apollo kicked him in the stomach, sending him toppling backward.

"I'm not the child you used to pick on, Ares. You want to fight me, I'm right here."

"Stop," River whispered. Her heartbeat sounded in her ears, and then it beat faster. "Stop!"

Everything went quiet, and both men stilled as they turned to her. Her heart galloped so fast she thought it might burst from her ribcage.

Twins. Identical twins.

"Princess," said Theo. "What is going on? What happened?"

She shook her head. "I… I'm not…"

"Tell him," Ares bellowed. "Tell this pompous asshole you're my mate."

River nodded. "I… I am, but…" She looked between Ares' bloodied chest and Apollo's bloodied face. He, too, looked angry, but more he looked… concerned. He called to her somewhere deep inside. The sight of Apollo in pain made her wolf whimper and want to soothe him.

She crossed to Apollo, and his cologne surrounded her. A forest floor after a spring rain. Heady and piney.

Again, her wolf howled.

River pushed a dark strand of hair from his forehead. Something tightened inside her.

Ares snarled, but she couldn't look away from Apollo as the blackness seeped out of his eyes as he took her in.

Mine. My Alpha.

It wasn't possible. There wasn't one of them, but two?

River closed her eyes and shook her head.

"What?" asked Ares. "Tell him you are my mate, River."

River nodded and turned back to Ares. Her gut twisted at the confused and hurt expression in his eyes, and she almost couldn't form the words.

"Yes. I am your mate, Ares. But…" She turned to Apollo, who stared at her as if she were the most fascinating thing he'd ever seen. "But somehow… I'm his mate, too."

The Story Continues in Book Two - Alpha Claimed

ALPHA CLAIMED

LYCAN KING WARS BOOK TWO

USA TODAY BESTSELLING AUTHOR

REBEKAH R. GANIERE

CHAPTER 1

RIVER

River sat at a large, highly polished wooden table. At one head seat sat Ares, and on the opposite side, Apollo sat in the head seat. River sat between them, with over five seats on either side of her. Across from her sat three older Lycans, all members of the Elder Council. The men stared at her, making her wolf pace uncomfortably.

"May I call you River, Highness?" asked one Elder.

"No," Ares and Apollo said together.

The tension in the air grew so thick that River didn't think she could have bitten through it with her fangs.

Her wolf whined, looking from Ares to Apollo and back again.

"Highness," repeated the Elder. "I am Osmodius, High Elder and uncle to Ares and Apollo. I welcome you to our lands and your new home."

River nodded and fiddled with the seam on her jeans.

"Highness, can you please try to explain what you are feeling?"

"Confused."

He nodded. "I'm sure you are. We all are."

"Is it even possible?" she asked. "That I could be both of their mates?"

Osmodius looked between the brothers and sighed. "It's... not unheard of, but it's exceedingly rare. But then, so are identical twins."

Ares slammed his fist into the table. "This is bullshit. She's mine. She said she's mine. I know she's mine."

Osmodius held up his hand. "I understand. But it is possible that you are not the only one she is right for."

"Tell them," Ares said. "Tell them you are mine, Beloved."

River looked at her hands. "It's true I did accept Ares."

"But he hasn't marked her," Apollo said. "That means the bond hasn't been completed."

River didn't like the pit that grew in her stomach as each moment passed.

"It's only because, due to my status, we knew that it was important to do things in the traditional manner," said Ares.

"But it hasn't been completed," Apollo said again.

Ares growled, and she glanced up at him. More than anything, she wished she could feel the comfort of his touch. As if sensing her distress, he stood and stepped toward her.

Apollo stood as well and growled. "Don't."

"Let's not get blood on your mother's favorite table, please," said Osmodius.

The brothers looked at each other, and then they both sat at the same time.

Identical faces. Identical mannerisms. Identical personalities.

Great. Just great. River didn't have just one overbearing Alpha to deal with; she had two. She wanted to run away. To get on her motorcycle and ride back to New York.

Oh, wait. She didn't have her motorcycle. *Dammit.*

Man… when her mom found out…

She sighed.

"I think there is only one good way to settle this," said Osmodius. "We must let Her Highness decide which mate to take."

She looked to Ares. He smiled at her in triumph.

Ares. She chose Ares.

"Wait!" Apollo yelled. "It's not fair. He's had an entire week with her. She doesn't know me at all. If you make her choose now, I don't stand a chance."

"Then I challenge you for her," said Ares.

"Wow!" said Apollo. "You are willing to give her up so easily, brother?"

Ares' fangs descended. "No. I'm ready to kill you to have her."

"Enough," said Osmodius. "The choice must be Her Highness's. But Apollo is right. To make her choose now would be unfair. Therefore, we will give her one month to make a decision. One month to spend with both of you and decide between you."

"That still gives him the advantage," said Apollo. "He's already had a week with her. Her bond with him is stronger. How can I compete with that?"

"If you don't think you can win her over, you can always relinquish your claim now."

"Not on your life," Apollo growled.

Osmodius looked at the other two elders, and they nodded.

"Very well. We will give Apollo one additional week to spend with her."

"Alone," said Apollo.

Ares jumped to his feet. "Absolutely not."

"What? Are you afraid that, away from your Alpha-hole ways, she might pick me?"

Ares grabbed the table's edge, and River could feel him hanging on by a thread.

"All right," she said.

All eyes turned to her.

"I'll do it. I'll spend time with Prince Apollo for four days."

"A week," Apollo corrected.

"Ares and I didn't spend a full week together in New York. He had meetings most days and was gone quite a bit." She wasn't about to tell Apollo or the elders that he'd moved into a different hotel room for four of the days and that she'd hidden from him for a day and a half.

"And she had a guard with her at all times. I want Zeke to go with them."

"No," said Apollo. "We'll take Silas and Bennett."

"No," Ares bellowed.

"Five days," said Osmodius. "You may pick which days-"

"Now," said Apollo. "Right now."

"She's just arrived and needs time to adjust," said Ares.

"Which is why it should be right now. Before she gets too cozy with you here at the estate." Apollo looked to Osmodius.

"I'd like Lachlan to come," River said. "Zeke and Bianca are trying to settle things back in the States so she can move here. I wouldn't want to take him away from her. But Lachlan... I would feel comfortable if he came." She hoped that her inference about how Apollo was taking her away so soon wouldn't go unnoticed.

"I would be honored," Lachlan stepped forward.

"Agreed," the other two said in unison.

"Where are you taking her?" Ares asked.

"Why? You gonna show up?"

"No. Because someone should know where she is in case you don't bring her back."

"We will make sure he leaves the address with us," said Osmodius.

"Fine. But at least let her eat before leaving," said Ares. "She hasn't eaten in hours."

"We can get something on the way." Apollo stood. "And no need to pack; we can get whatever we need when we get there."

River's heart hammered, and her hands shook. They talked about her like she wasn't even in the room, and that she wouldn't have. Yes, they may have just decided that she had to spend time with Apollo, but her life was still her own, and if she wanted to, she could just walk out the door and tell them all to screw themselves, and there was nothing they could do about it.

"I want to eat now," she blurted. "And change my clothes. And pee."

The men looked at her, and Osmodius nodded. "Of course, Highness. Take as long as you need."

"One hour," said Apollo.

"Two," she countered. "If I am about to go to an undisclosed location in a foreign country with a man I don't even know, the least you can do is give me two hours to prepare."

"Agreed," said one of the elders.

Her shoulders relaxed a fraction.

Osmodius looked at his watch. "Very well. Please be ready by five p.m., Highness."

Apollo burst from the room and disappeared. River waited until the three elders left before running to Ares and being swept into his arms. He kissed her head, and she held back a sob. Just when she'd gotten used to the idea of being his mate, she had to start all over again with someone else. It felt worse than cheating. Despite Apollo's pull on her wolf, she'd already made her choice.

"I don't want to go."

Ares kissed her hair again and pulled her even closer. "I don't want you to."

"Why do I have to go with him? Why can't they just let us be?"

Ares stiffened. "Because… He is the Alpha of Alphas."

She stepped back and looked up at him. "The what?"

Ares blew out a breath. "The Alpha of Alphas. When more than one Alpha is born into the family, it falls on the oldest to take charge. He was given the title of Alpha of Alphas."

"But… you're twins."

"And he's five minutes older."

"Five minutes? Are you joking? They are basing all of this on five minutes?" The fate of her future came down to Apollo evacuating his mother's womb first.

"I am not the Alpha of Alphas. I am only second in line. Therefore, they have to give him a chance. They have no choice. Alphas need mates, and their mates need to bear pups. Apollo and I are way past the age where we should have found you. As much as I hate it with every hair on my body, they must give him a chance. If you are indeed his fated mate as you are mine, then not giving him a chance would go against everything we believe in."

"But… I don't want him," she whispered.

Ares cupped her face and kissed her. "Believe me, I don't want you to want him, Beloved."

ARES

ARES TRIED TO KEEP FROM LOSING IT IN FRONT OF RIVER. JUST THE thought of her alone in the company of another male, especially his brother, scared him more than words could describe.

His whole life, Apollo had tried to take everything Ares cared about. Their father's affection. Then their mother's. And now his fated mate's.

They lay on his bed, wrapped in each other's arms, listening to the clock ticking on the wall. She'd not spoken in almost thirty minutes, and the tension in her posture told him everything he needed to know.

"Tell me something about yourself," she said into his chest. "Something… special."

Special? What was special about him?

He thought for a moment. "When I was young, I used to have a favorite blanket. I took it everywhere with me. One day, it disappeared. I was devastated. My mother had made me the blanket out of her nightgowns."

River squeezed him. "Do you know what happened to it?"

"I have a pretty good idea." *Apollo.*

A knock on the door pulled their attention, and Ares looked at the clock. Four fifty-five.

"Come," he called.

Lachlan opened the door and peeked inside. "It's time, Highnesses."

"We're coming."

His wolf snarled and paced so hard that every ounce of his body focused on not shifting.

"I should go," she said. "I don't want to make him mad."

Ares tipped her chin, so she looked at him. "Who cares if it does?"

"I don't want him to hurt you again."

"If he hurts *you* in any way, I will kill him. Elders or no elders."

She gave him a sad smile and then slid off the bed. Ares rose as well, but she stopped him.

"No. I don't want you to see this."

"River-"

She ran to him, slammed her lips into his, and quickly broke away.

"I should have let you mark me. I should have asked you last night."

His heart shattered at her confession, and he pulled her close. "No, Beloved. We both know that you would have regretted it later if you had. This is better."

Her eyes narrowed. "You don't mean that."

Did he? "I do," he finally said. "This way, when you choose me, there will be no doubt in your mind."

Dear Reader,

Thank you for taking the time to read *Alpha Marked.* I never thought I would write a reverse harem, but when this idea came into my head, I just could not let it go.

I hope you love Ares and Apollo as much as River will.

If you enjoyed the book, please take a moment to leave a review on your favorite retailer. Your reviews make all the difference to an author and the success of books.

Feel free to take a moment and email me and let me know what you liked about the book or who your favorite character was and why. I love hearing from readers. It makes writing so much more fun when I hear from my readers.

VampWereZombie@Gmail.com

To find out more about me and my Upcoming Releases, Please Join my Street Team for Swag and Freebies.

I also love connecting with readers! Stalk me everywhere!

I look forward to hearing from you!

Rebekah R. Ganiere - BOOKS WITH A BITE

USA Today Bestselling Author

Rebekah R. Ganiere

Fairelle Series

Red the Were Hunter - Book One

Yanti's Choice - Free Fairelle Short Story

Snow the Vampire Slayer - Book Two

Jamen's Yuletide Bride - Book Three

Zelle and the Tower - Book Four

Cinder the Fae - Book Five

Belle and the Beast - Book Six

Gerall's Festivus Bride - Book Seven

Jak the Giant Healer - Book Eight

Olivia and the Giant - Book Nine (Coming Soon)

Eric's Wayward Bride - Book Ten (Coming Soon)

Wolf River

PROMISED at the Moon

CURSED by the Moon

RECLAIMED from the Moon

TAMED under the Moon

UNLEASHED with the Moon

FATED despite the Moon

FOUND because of the Moon

The Society Series

Reign of the Vampires

Rise of the Fae

Vengeance of the Demons

The Otherworlder Series

Kidnapped at Christmas

Vigilante at Valentine

Massacre at Mardi Gras

Hoodwinked at Halloween

Nightmare at New Year (Coming Soon)

Immortal Monsters

Dracula's Bride

Frankenstein's Bride (Coming Soon)

Lycan King Wars

Alpha Marked

Alpha Claimed

Alpha Queen

God and Monsters Fated Mates

Thor

Loki

Fenrir

Tyr

Happy Holiday Romances

Rekindling Christmas

Christmas Lodge

Dead Awakenings

Kissed by the Reaper

NEWSLETTER

To claim your Two FREE Books and find out more about Rebekah R. Ganiere and her other Upcoming Releases
You can Go Here:
www.RebekahGaniere.com/Newsletter

www.ingramcontent.com/pod-product-compliance
Lightning Source LLC
LaVergne TN
LVHW091118080826
845145LV00008B/1969
9781633000919